A New Song

by the same author

The Enchanted Toby Jug
A Blazing Torch

A NEW SONG

by Eve Hanley

Illustrations by
Gustave Nebel

Weybright and Talley, Inc.
New York

To my sons Howard and Edward and
to my friend Kate Goldie, with
fondest love.

Library of Congress Catalog Card Number: 68-12863

Published by Weybright and Talley, Inc.
3 East 54th Street, New York, N.Y. 10022

Printed in the United States of America

Contents

A New Song

I

'Those Staceys'

People, when they spoke of them, never called them 'the Staceys'; always 'those Staceys,' which suggested that as a family they were out of the ordinary run of families. This would have astonished the Staceys, if they had realized it. If they had thought about it at all, they would have considered themselves very commonplace.

They lived in an old brown house on the outskirts of London. The house was draughty, inconvenient and shabby, but it was roomy. It needed to be, since there were four Stacey children, as well as a dog.

Because it was oldish, too, the house had a far larger garden than usual nowadays. The garden was a wilderness, but it had enchantment. A little spring bubbled up and made a channel through it, and delicate water plants and ferns grew on its banks. There were apple trees in the garden, and a row of poplars grew at the bottom, tall and tempting.

'Race you to the poplars!' the Stacey children had always cried to each other. And when that race was run—'Race you up the tallest poplar! Race you to the mark!' The mark was a blaze on the trunk of the tallest poplar which their father had cut as a warning to them, for their own safety, to go no further. 'Children sometimes fall out of trees and hurt themselves,' he had said gravely. But that had been when the children were very young. Now they were old enough to have common sense about climbing, and only go up as far as was safe, anyway.

'I think poplars are the very best trees, and ours are the very best poplars!' panted Alix, throwing herself down in the long grass after a climb. She was the youngest of the four and climbed the most nowadays.

'They're not the easiest,' said Christopher. He was the eldest: climbing was becoming rather beneath his dignity, but he had had a great deal of experience. 'Yews are easier, because of the side branches growing low. And oaks—'

'Oh, oaks!' cried Tessa. 'I wish—I *wish* we had an oak tree in our garden!'

'It would be convenient for Oak-apple Day,' Alix agreed. 'We could gather oak-apples for the birthday.' The birthday was the shared birthday of Mr. and Mrs. Stacey: May 29th, Oak-apple Day. Mr. Stacey always said that the discovery of the tremendous coincidence of their birthdays, when they were courting, had finally decided them upon marriage.

'It would be interesting to try to make ink from the galls,' said Billy. 'I believe you can.'

'What galls?' Tessa asked.

Patiently, 'Oak-apples are galls. It's just another name. They're not fruit at all; they're abnormal growths made by gall-wasps—'

'Stop it, Billy!' Tessa said loudly, 'I don't want to know. I just like to think they're there for the birthday, and how romantic it is that they're worn in memory of Bonnie Prince Charlie who hid in the oak tree and escaped—'

'You've got it all wrong, Tessa,' said Christopher. 'Muddled up Charles II and Bonnie Prince Charlie, just to make it more romantic—'

'And won't listen about gall-wasps,' said Billy.

'Oh, you!' cried Tessa, rolling over in the grass away from them so that she could not hear.

'Listen! Listen!' The voice of Alix which had to shout, even in peace making, rose above them. 'It doesn't matter. Because we haven't any oaks; but we have the best poplars in the world—and I'm going to climb the tallest again—now!'

And up she went, and Billy raced with her; but Christopher lounged in a grown-up way among the grasses, and Tessa still lay with her head buried, wishing that Bonnie Prince Charles and Charles II had been the same, wishing they had a centuries-old oak-tree in the garden, wishing—as usual—all kinds of impossible things.

The poplars were not their only trees, however, and because the garden was large and overgrown, with welcoming bushes and trees, there were always birds. Thrushes and blackbirds sang all through the Spring; and whatever the season, there was singing inside the Stacey's house—at least, when Mrs. Stacey was at home. For Mrs. Stacey was a singer and a teacher of singing. She was small and demure-looking—quite different in appearance from what most people seem to expect of a singer. She gave recitals and sang in oratorios, so that she was more often out of the house than in it. When she was at home she was usually in the music room teaching pupils, or practicing her own singing. Then Tessa was usually with her, as accompanist.

Tessa, next to Christopher in age, wanted to become a concert pianist. She had always wanted it; she still did; but both her parents were against the idea. They had good reasons, she knew, although they seldom pressed them. One morning she had been practicing. She looked up, and there they stood in the doorway. Her mother was looking out of the window, down the garden, to where the slender poplars moved against the sunlight. But Tessa knew that she had been listening intently and now was only looking away because she was thinking.

Her father was looking directly at her, and said, as though they were in the middle of a conversation : 'Always practise as though for a performance, Tessa.' Then he added, 'You can give small recitals when you grow up, but you should go in for teaching.'

'Teaching!' said Tessa. 'I want to be a concert pianist— you know that.'

Her mother was looking at her now. 'Oh, Tessa!' She sighed with a real regret. 'For that you would need the strength of an ox and the tenacity of a bull dog. Certainly you're no bull dog by nature.'

Tessa hung her head. She wanted to be at the top, but was not eager for the relentless grind necessary to get herself there. She was lazy—in her more honest moments, she knew it.

Besides, what about strength? Her mother had not said where the strength of the ox was lacking; but everyone knew she was always the one in the family to go down with colds and headaches. Her headaches were no ordinary ones, either : they were blinding, disabling attacks. Mrs. Stacey said that her mother—the children's grandmother—had suffered from the same kind of thing. It must run in families.

So, 'Give small recitals and go in for teaching,' Mr. Stacey repeated.

'Ugh!' said Tessa.

'Well, if it's to be music, that's how it will have to be. You're good at ensemble, after all; but you haven't the stuff of a soloist.'

Tessa could not argue. Her father knew what he was talking about. He played the cello in a London orchestra; he was also choir master and organist at their parish church.

All the Staceys were musical—'Music-mad' some of the neighbours said sourly, adding, 'Those Staceys!'

2

Two Exceptions

Mr. and Mrs. Stacey were professional musicians and they knew how hard that livelihood could turn out to be. They were both unusually gifted, and yet they had been—and still were—having to scrape together every penny. Bringing up a family of four—not to speak of Chip, the dog—was an expensive matter, at the best of times. The Staceys' parents would not lightly encourage any of their children to take up a musical career.

Not Tessa—certainly not Tessa.

Nor Christopher, who played both organ and viola. He composed too. He was gifted, certainly, but he had other gifts that were perhaps greater. He was doing well at school, especially in mathematics. He could specialize in that, perhaps win a university scholarship—there were many possible careers for him besides music. Christopher, who was even-tempered and reasonable, was beginning to see the sense of all this.

And Billy, who played the violin, did not even think of becoming a professional musician, anyway. Botany, not music, was his first love. In his dreams there were no concert platforms, no awed silence, followed by thunderous applause. Instead he dreamed that he walked in Kew Gardens, prowling watchfully along the flower beds and through the great glass houses, *a member of the staff*.

Lastly Alix, the youngest of the family—yes, her parents judged that she really had both the musical gifts and the temperament that would have made a musical career possible. And Alix did not want it. She played the oboe: 'I love the oboe,' she said. 'I really love it. I'll practice and practice, and I'll play whenever people want me to. Oh, yes—all that! But I must—I *must* be a nurse.'

A nurse! Tessa gazed at her young sister with a mixture of envy and amazement: envy of the great musical gift that she herself lacked; amazement that its owner could seem so to undervalue its possession. Above all, Tessa could not understand why Alix should want to nurse at all.

But Alix loved to bring order out of disorder, comfort out of discomfort. That was at least partly what appealed to her in nursing. Her own family gave her a certain scope. She did—or tried to do—all the things that her mother was too busy to attend to. In his wife's frequent absences Mr. Stacey saw to it, as far as possible, that all the children had their regular jobs about the house; but Alix mothered the whole family, including her parents.

'That child!' said Mrs. Bullock, who came in to help with the cleaning. She felt that Alix was on her side in the housework and all that went with it; but at the same time she felt indignant that 'the poor thing' was put upon. But Alix was no 'poor thing'; she chose to do what she did, and liked it. It was she who darned the boys' socks and sewed on buttons. She knew where clean handkerchiefs were to be found. She reminded her mother when it was time for her concert dresses to be cleaned. She ran up and down stairs with hot drinks when Tessa was in bed with one of her colds. And when Tessa was not in bed but leaning her head on her hand, white-faced, dazed, dumb, Alix would whisper, 'If it's one of your headaches, Tess, then you'd be far better in bed. Look—leave everything. I'll clear up. You go upstairs now. And I'll be up with some aspirin by the time you're in bed.'

So, in her way, Alix seemed to have everything she wanted: her oboe, and her family to look after in the present; and in the future the profession of nursing was waiting for her. There is always a great need for nurses.

Everything she wanted, with perhaps two exceptions.

The first was a dog. There was already one dog in the house, Chip, and everyone liked him and he liked everybody—he was that kind of dog. But he belonged to Billy—or you could put it the other way about: Billy belonged to him. Alix observed wistfully the closeness of the companionship. That was what she wanted: a dog of her *own*—the responsibility as well as the pleasure of it. Every morning Billy was up early to exercise Chip before going to school. Alix got up early, too, for her household chores; but she would have liked to have had to get up even earlier to exercise a dog as well. On Billy's return for breakfast, Chip bounced in and danced eagerly round Alix as she bustled about, but she was never deceived: that was the friendliness he showed to everyone. Really and truly he was Billy's dog; Billy was his god.

Alix would never have voiced her longings; but Tessa happened once to remark bluntly, 'Why should Billy be the only one to have a dog?'

'Oh!' said Alix. 'You can't want Billy *not* to have Chip?'

'No, but—'

'—But why shouldn't we each have a dog?' asked Christopher, ever logical.

Alix's eyes had become round with amazement and delight at the idea. 'A dog each? Do you really think we might?'

But their parents, consulted, flatly said no. 'Chip's big enough and hungry enough as it is. We simply couldn't afford to feed three more dogs.'

Mrs. Stacey added: 'What would they all be doing when I'm teaching in the music room? And when you're all at school, and your father and I both out?'

Tessa still grumbled: 'But I don't see why not, when Billy has a dog.'

Mr. Stacey said patiently, 'If there were a great need for any one of you three to have a dog, in the same way as you need food or clothes, then no doubt your mother and I would try to provide you with one. But there is no such need. As for Billy, do you grudge him his piece of good fortune?'

Billy's good fortune had been the result of some rock-gardening in his spare time for old Mr. Baker down the road. Billy had offered his services free—'for the experience,' he had said earnestly. There had been no mention of cash payment; but at the end Mr. Baker had presented him with a puppy. 'A chip off the old block,' Mr. Baker had said; but which block nobody quite knew. However, Mr. Baker, being the local timber merchant, must know all about chips and blocks.

Bella, Chip's mother, looked mostly bassett hound. For years before Chip's birth she had had two devoted husbands: a Labrador and an Aberdeen. Which was Chip's father? It was impossible to say. Alix studied the question, and studied all Bella's litters as they came. By now Bella had added a third mate—a Jack Russell. Each fresh batch of puppies was a source of speculation. Would they be small or large dogs, fluffy or smooth? Would they have mournful eyes and pricked ears, or floppy ears and a saucy expression? And whom would they go to, as master or mistress?

To this last question Alix knew with certainty a part of the answer : not to Alix Stacey.

And the second thing that Alix lacked? Sometimes— very occasionally—her own family became too much for her. Or, rather, their way of life did. The house was so shabby, untidy; the household so often in breathless confusion. She made great efforts to get things straight, and to keep them so. She was aided by Mrs.Bullock in a rather defeatist spirit. Their efforts had some effect, but never a permanent one. Alix constantly fought a battle which as constantly she seemed upon the point of losing.

So, of all the family, Alix was the one who most enjoyed going on a visit to Aunt Elizabeth's. She loved the quiet orderliness, the routine that could be relied upon, the neatness and cleanness and *mended-right-up-to-dateness* of the household.

The invitation from Aunt Elizabeth and Uncle Robert usually came for the Easter or summer holidays, and was for two children. ('Why does she order us in pairs?' Tessa had once asked, in a rebellious moment. But, as no one dared put that question to Aunt Elizabeth herself, the answer could never be known.)

This time the invitation was for Alix and Billy—with Chip, of course.

'We much look forward to seeing Alix and Billy again'— Mrs.Stacey was reading aloud from her elder sister's letter to the family at the breakfast table. *'No doubt Alix will find things she wants to do in the house, as last time; and Billy will want to work in the garden. This time he will meet Alfred—'*

'Who's Alfred?' asked Billy.

'If you'll let your mother go on reading . . .' said Mr. Stacey mildly.

Mrs. Stacey smiled and continued : 'Aunt Elizabeth just says : '*—meet Alfred, who has begun helping regularly in the garden. This is a great boon, as neither Robert nor I are as good at stooping and kneeling nowadays as gardeners need to be. . . .*' And that's really the end of the letter, except for train times for you to choose from. Oh! and a P.S. to say that Captain McIvor is well.' Captain McIvor was Aunt Elizabeth's large and beautiful ginger cat.

Alix said nothing to the letter, but sighed happily.

Billy looked uneasy—and not merely at the thought of keeping Chip and Captain McIvor apart; that was an old problem, and he had become skilled at finding answers to it in the past. No, the new and mysterious presence in the garden troubled him. 'Some gardeners are awfully bossy and don't-touch : do you think Alfred Whoeveritis may be like that?'

'No,' said Christopher, with the reassuring judgment of an elder brother. 'Aunt Elizabeth's not like that, and she's not likely to let anyone like that into her garden.'

'I hope you're right,' said Billy somberly.

3

The Music of the Morning

Aunt Elizabeth was an imposing person with long slender feet which turned slightly outwards as she walked. She was much older than Mrs. Stacey, and the Stacey children were rather afraid of her sometimes; but sometimes, too, she had a dimple which appeared even when she wasn't smiling. And once Tessa had heard her say energetically to Uncle Robert that something was 'Bilge.' Not a very strong expression in itself, perhaps, but certainly unexpected from someone like Aunt Elizabeth. Chris, to whom the exclamation was reported, had said, 'Impossible! Not Aunt *Elizabeth*!' But Tessa declared that she had not been mistaken, and Aunt Elizabeth went up a notch in the children's estimation.

She and Uncle Robert lived right in the country, on the edge of the downland. They hadn't even a telephone, although that was really a matter of choice rather than of remoteness. The two of them always reminded Alix of those people who live in a toy house that tells the weather. On fine days Aunt Elizabeth, in a stately wide-brimmed hat, would come into the garden; and on wet ones Uncle Robert, mackintoshed and umbrellaed, would emerge to do the shopping.

Those stately hats of Aunt Elizabeth's! Both sisters constantly wore hats, but the difference between them!—

Alix mused on it sometimes, when her mother was in church, about to sing. Alix would be waiting to accompany her—like a little blackbird to follow with her oboe her mother's glorious blackbird voice. People in the congregation were astonished when first they heard that voice issuing from the small body, which was always topped by a flat, squashed-looking hat. The children said that, if the skies split and the moon and stars clashed together, their mother would reach for just such a hat.

Such a hat was unthinkable for Aunt Elizabeth. Not for her, either, a wobbly, timid bunch of violets trembling on the brim. She liked velvet roses, curled and beautiful, like the ones in her own garden.

Aunt Elizabeth had no interest in music and seldom listened to it: she had never really grasped the fact that her little sister was a public figure in a world that was strange to her. This annoyed Billy, but, as Alix sensibly pointed out, unless you were tremendously famous, as Winston Churchill had been, thousands of people who were not interested in your pursuits might never have heard of you. Alix and Billy were passing the time in such discussion as they sat in the train that was taking them to visit Aunt Elizabeth.

'Still,' said Billy, pondering Alix's argument, 'Aunt Elizabeth must *know* about Mother's concerts and things. I mean, she must know they go on. You'd think it would make her realize. Instead of which she just thinks Mother's not very keen on housekeeping. And she only thinks about Father's being hard up; she doesn't seem to realize that he's a first class musician too. Oh! and she's an awful snob.'

'A snob?'

'Well, you've only to see her with Chip. Just because he's

not pure bred, like Captain McIvor; and I'd rather have a nice mixed dog any day than—'

'But Aunt Elizabeth is the kind of person who prefers cats to dogs.'

'Anyway,' said Billy, 'I wouldn't bring Chip except that the visit does him good—the fresh air of the country, I mean. But the way Aunt Elizabeth looks at him! And when she does say anything—!'

Aunt Elizabeth had once said that Chip smelt, and stared at him regally over what the Stacey children called her 'corsfiage.' This meant her trim blouse, which jutted forward to curve in again to a slim waist. Chip himself always seemed to sense that these were grace and favour holidays, and kept out of Aunt Elizabeth's way—and Captain McIvor's—as much as possible.

'But don't forget that she does invite Chip, as well as us, of her own free will,' pursued Alix. And, unwilling to let the charge of snobbery pass altogether: 'She may be a bit of a snob in her way; but she hasn't all that money, you know. And yet she always manages to look like—like a duchess. I rather admire people who can do that.'

'Well, I don't see the point of it,' said Billy stubbornly.

'And she's a marvellous gardener.'

The train whistled as it entered the last tunnel before their station.

Billy's defiance turned to gloom as he remembered something. 'And now the gardening's going to be done by this Alfred.'

'Don't be silly,' said Alix with conviction, beginning to gather the luggage. 'Remember what Chris said. Aunt Elizabeth would always be in charge. When you talk to Alfred for the first time, you'll find that out at once, I'm sure of it.'

Billy peered out of the carriage window as they drew up to the station platform. He was keeping a sharp, suspicious eye open for any forbidding male figure who might turn out to be Alfred. Nobody more alarming than Uncle Robert, beaming a welcome, was to be seen.

In fact, it was Alix who was the first Stacey to talk to Alfred Stevens.

On the morning after her arrival with Billy and Chip, Alix was downstairs early to practice her oboe before breakfast. She had opened the French windows to let in the sunny morning air, and suddenly she became aware of being listened to—of being watched. It was the same feeling she had when Captain McIvor was in the room, without her having known it at first.

She looked round. Just outside the window, leaning on a hoe with which he had been at work, stood a large young man with gentle eyes and an even gentler smile curling his mouth. He did not hurry to speak, but as though he had known her all her life, and as though they had often discussed her playing and her future, he said, 'You must play that pipe for people to enjoy, when you grow up.'

And, as directly, Alix had replied : 'I want to be a hospital nurse.'

He shook his head slowly. 'There's plenty could be nurses, but not many who can play a little wooden pipe like an angel straight from the Lord's own music makers.'

'You're Mr. Stevens,' said Alix, realizing that introductions had been by-passed.

'I'm Alf,' he agreed.

Alf was the last of the large Stevens family, and his mother always said that the wits had been running out by the time he was born; but, to make up, he had been given an extra allowance of sweet nature. She had brought him up very

religiously, on church and Bible and hymn book, and all
his thinking and ways of expression showed it.

He had tried several jobs since leaving school—in a gar-

age, in a shop, and so on: his employers always said that
he was willing but far too slow; and Alf himself had been
unhappy. Then he began gardening for Aunt Elizabeth, and
everything had changed. He was still slow-thinking and
slow-moving, but Aunt Elizabeth—who had the highest

standards, after all—seemed to find this no great drawback. 'He never injures a plant, and *he learns all the time*,' she said emphatically, and that was that.

So Alf Stevens became a happy worker in Aunt Elizabeth's garden, and happiest of all when the Stacey children were there. He and Billy worked together at weeding and digging, composting and pruning, and all the other jobs with Aunt Elizabeth in supervision and command like a captain on the bridge. But any jobs that needed doing near the house were saved bv Alf for the times when Alix would be practicing on her 'little wooden pipe.' Thus he heard her music often.

The early morning, before most people's breakfast, had always been Alf's choice of time to start in the garden. Now, for the Stacey children, he sometimes came at dawn itself. There was a special reason for that. Alf knew all the birds and birdsong of the countryside and talked to the children about them. 'They pipe like Miss Alix,' he said, 'but they begin even earlier. You should hear 'em. Heavenly music they make, all together, with the very first of the morning. Then quieten again, so that nobody knows of it.'

'You mean the dawn chorus?' said Alix.

'I don't know the name for it,' said Alf; 'but heavenly music with the dawn—that's it.'

'We've heard of the dawn chorus,' said Billy, 'but never been up in time for it.'

'Do you think—?' asked Alix.

'I'll wake you,' promised Alf.

So the next morning there was a soft rattle of gravel, first on Alix's window, then on Billy's. Only a little later and before it was fully light, the children stole out of the house, with Chip at their heels—out, with Alf, into the white mists of very early morning—ground mists like a feathery lake. Above, the sky was clear and steel blue and wore, pinned to its breast, a blazing star.

They brushed through the wet, heavy grass until they came to the wood at the bottom of the garden, and there they waited, quiet as lizards, shivering with the chill of sunlessness. Chip shivered too, with desire to be on the move, but Billy's quiet hand was on his collar.

Then it began. Usually a blackbird's note first: slow, almost as though he were trying his voice. Then other blackbirds, thrushes, robins, finches, a cuckoo—until the whole wood sang. . . .

At last the four of them turned back to the house, still long before either Aunt Elizabeth or Uncle Robert were ready to come out to 'tell the weather.' Both aunt and uncle knew of these early expeditions. At first Aunt Elizabeth had been inclined to forbid them: there was such risk of chill, she said. Uncle Robert retorted briskly, 'Don't fuss, Elizabeth. There is no risk that an extra layer of wool will not deal with.' So that was that; and again and again Alix and Billy heard their music of the morning, among the trees.

On their return once, Alix said, 'It's a wild wood, but it couldn't be better if anyone had tried to make it. I mean, if they had planted it specially. The birds must love it. And do you know, I'm sure there's an oak in it—on the far side.'

'There are three,' said Billy. 'I counted. And Alf says there are often galls—oak-apples—too. He says they really are there on the birthday.'

'We must tell Tess and Chris,' said Alix happily.

They told the other two not only about the oak trees and the oak-apples but also about the dawn chorus, and above all about Alf Stevens, who had opened such gateways for them. So the other pair of Stacey children felt they knew Alf even before they met him. When they actually met him, on the next holiday, they stepped at once into friendship. All the Stacey children became Alf's friends.

4

The Well House,
the Bookroom, Still Life,
and Other Things

Alix had always loved going to Aunt Elizabeth's. She remembered going when she was so small that she could sit
comfortably under the kitchen table, arranging all Aunt
Elizabeth's little herb boxes in their special order.

Later, she had invented a special game called Tigrunting—a portmanteau word for tiger hunting—which she
and Captain McIvor played together. This was in Captain
McIvor's youth, before he grew heavy and slow-moving
and on his dignity; it was in the years before Chip was
born. Tigrunting was played upstairs in the evening, with
all the lights turned out. Alix would crawl stealthily about the
landings and bedrooms; Captain McIvor would wait his
moment, then pounce out from behind a door and pat her
in the face—no claws exposed—and then dash off to hide
somewhere else.

And then there had always been the visits to the well
house, as it was called—an ancient stone structure at the
end of the garden which contained a well, complete with
windlass and bucket. Long, long ago, this had supplied the
household with its water; and Uncle Robert kept the chain

renewed and the whole apparatus working because it was useful for the watering of the garden. The children had never been allowed to go into the well house alone : the well was deep and therefore dangerous. Nowadays they could go in the company of Alf when he went to fill his watering can and buckets. It was exciting to enter the damp, dark little place in Alf's reassuring company and to peer over the low wall into those terrifying depths. You were often glad for someone to be holding on to your jersey or shirt. If you dropped a stone down the well shaft, quite a time elapsed before you heard the distant *falop*.

Christopher was rather above the pleasures of Alix and Billy, but Uncle Robert had recently begun inviting him to make use of his bookroom, as he called it—a great honor. This was a tiny room, too small to be called a library, but containing a very large number of books, for every wall was a bookcase from floor to ceiling. Christopher seemed to find a little of everything—except modern novels, for Uncle Robert believed those were for borrowing, not for owning. And when Christopher tired of reading, with his long legs stretched out on the shabby old horsehair settee, then he would wander out of the house and through the garden and the garden gate and across the meadow by the bridle path to the little parish church. Here there was an organ on which he was welcome to practice whenever he liked, and he often did.

It seemed as if Tessa might be the one to find least enjoyment in a visit to Aunt Elizabeth. She herself said that it almost gave her a nervous breakdown, trying to be tidy. Yet, even so, she found an odd satisfaction in the discipline of the household. And she loved Uncle Robert. He was a busy, trotting little man, a churchwarden. He played bowls and dabbled in painting. Tessa liked to arrange still life for him to paint—once it was a slender wineglass, a lemon, and two onions on a piece of ruffled purple silk. One onion was in its golden skin, the other peeled, showing its purple veins.

'Altogether terribly difficult!' said Uncle Robert with relish. 'I like the transparency of the glass against the dark background. And peeled onions are such delicate things. . . .'

Aunt Elizabeth had come in. 'I hope you are aware, Robert, that that wineglass is over a hundred years old.'

'Perfectly aware, my dear,' replied Uncle Robert, busily collecting his painting materials. Tessa thought he resembled a sparrow, hopping around, picking a crumb here, a crumb there; and Aunt Elizabeth looked like a very stately pigeon.

Tessa laughed silently at the thought and went to make the salad for lunch. Aunt Elizabeth stayed with Uncle Robert for a while, fussing affectionately over his preparations for painting. She came back into the kitchen just as Tessa was beginning to jumble the ingredients of the salad together. She gave a little scream: 'Not like *that*! Food should not only be good, it should *look* attractive. First line the bowl with lettuce leaves. Now the peas and beans. Now an edging of tomato rings. The beets are so very small that they can go in whole. Then a few chopped walnuts—and there you are! If you can arrange a still life for a painter as good as your uncle, surely you can make a pretty salad. . . .'

Tessa stood back and looked at what the salad had now become. It certainly looked pretty. 'We don't do things like that at home,' she said. 'The boys are always so hungry they'd eat anything, and Father bolts his food, talking all the time. Mother's meals are hopelessly erratic. She never eats anything at all before singing in public. She just has a glass of milk and honey.'

Aunt Elizabeth blew through her elegant nostrils. It was

5
'If only. . . .'

The good-weather holidays which the Staceys did not spend with Aunt Elizabeth and Uncle Robert they usually spent at home, and mostly out of doors.

Their garden was as different from Aunt Elizabeth's as could be imagined. There was no money to employ anyone like Alf Stevens to work in it. Mr. and Mrs. Stacey had no time to spare for it at all; the children did what they could, but that was not much. Unlike their parents, however, they did not regret the neglect of the garden. It ran wild, and they loved it that way.

'I only wish——' began Tessa.

'You and your only-wishes!' said Chris good-humoredly.

'I *only* wish we had a well house or something mysterious like that,' said Tessa; 'but otherwise—truly—there's nothing from Aunt Elizabeth's garden that I really *need* in ours.'

Billy agreed with her. In spite of the fascination of Aunt Elizabeth's alpines and other exotic plants, he preferred their own garden. He brooded lovingly, with more than a botanist's interest, over the blue of the self-sown forget-me-nots and the golden kingcups along the banks of their stream.

'If only the stream were a little deeper, though,' sighed Tessa.

'Couldn't we dig it deeper?' suggested Alix. She was

34

ready at a word to fetch a spade and begin. But Chris, who
knew about such things, said briefly, 'Sides would fall in.'

So they contented themselves with paddling and potter-
ing about in the depths that had been granted to them; and
in summer pitched a tent so that they could fall asleep
lulled by the sound of their own stream. Mr. and Mrs. Stacey
thought theirs was most natural behaviour. The neighbours
said it was positively wicked to let children sleep so near to
water: those Stacey children would fall victim to rheuma-
tism and other diseases of dampness.

Certainly Tessa caught colds, but never from camping.
'Poor things!' she said of the neighbours, with real pity.
To them the Staceys' enchanting stream was only a kind
of undesirable dampness on the move. They suspected and
feared its presence on their own properties. For the stream,
when it left the Staceys' garden, lost freedom and charm
together; it was piped, and houses had been built over it.

Chip didn't like it when they camped. He had to stop
indoors in the kitchen at night. Otherwise he was apt to
rush out of the tent in order to be able to bark properly at
cats or hedgehogs, and then no one had any sleep. 'That
Stacey dog!' the neighbours said.

Sometimes it would rain, and the children would hear
the drops patter like beads on the canvas. Only once were
they driven in. That night blue lightning seemed to be about
to hit the tent, and the thunder—so close upon it—had a
roaring, ripping sound, as though someone were tearing
gigantic strips of calico.

'Of course, we're not frightened,' Alix had said at the
very beginning, and Tessa, looking at her, realized that
Alix had said that just because she was at least a little
afraid. Tessa felt surprise—and yet suddenly recognized
that her young sister was like that. 'Such a reliable little

thing!' Aunt Elizabeth always said of Alix. That was true, and yet Alix also had these sudden impulses of timidity— and of daring—just as though she tired occasionally of being reliable and responsible and grown-up beyond her years.

'Anyway, we're not the only people to be woken by it,' said Billy, trying to sound casual. Lights were popping up in all the houses. A window in their own was flung up, and the pyjamaed figure of Mr. Stacey leaned out into the rain to shout urgently: 'Inside! Inside—all of you—at once! Leave the tent! Quick!'

'Come on!' said Chris, backing his father's authority.

They seized their sleeping bags and made a dash across the garden, heads down against the rain. They had scarcely entered the house before there came a metallic bang from outside and an odd sulphurous smell. It was almost as if their father had known that something had been going to happen. In fact, one of the trees in a neighbouring garden had been struck—but the Staceys didn't know that for certain until the next morning.

'I wish it had been one of ours,' said Billy, when he heard the news. 'Lucky things!'

'Oh, Billy, not one of our poplars!' cried Alix.

'Just *one*,' said Billy.

'No! You can't mean it. *All* the poplars are special.'

'But just one—'

'Anyway,' Chris said to conclude the argument, 'it didn't happen.'

'Wouldn't it have been dramatic if it had . . .' said Tessa dreamily.

Fair weather or foul, the holidays passed. When they had gone, they seemed gone for good and all; term—and all the

routine and rush that went with it—started and seemed
determined to go on forever. Tessa always felt there was an
unfairness in that.

On the first day of the Spring term, Tessa woke cross.
She lay and looked at the sky, which seemed to be made of
dove's feathers, pink and grey. She knew she ought to get
up. Last night she had flounced from the room, after almost
quarrelling with her father. He had reproached her for her
desultory ways at school, hoping that she would do better
in the new term than in the previous one. He had said
that she must begin thinking ahead—thinking of how she
could eventually earn a living; and again he had brought
up the odious subject of teaching music.

Tessa lay in bed and listened to the bustling sounds of
the Stacey household starting its day. Suddenly she buried
her head in the pillow. Oh! If only she lived far, far away
from everyone in a little stone house all by herself. Remote,
but not so remote perhaps that she had no visitors. No, a
rich lady happening to wander by would hear Tessa's playing and be struck by her giftedness; she would waft Tessa to
London and there help her from triumph to triumph. . . .

Yes, but what she needed was that rich lady. . . . 'Father
sees I am well taught,' Tessa admitted grudgingly to herself; 'but in spite of all his contacts he doesn't do a thing
for me outside the family.'

'Are you feeling all right, Tess?' Alix had come into the
room.

Tessa raised a healthy, cross face from the pillow and
Alix, relieved, went on: 'You'll be late for school. Mother
has had breakfast already and has gone to Kensington to
teach.'

'Well, I always set breakfast overnight, don't I?'

'Yes, but do hurry up now, Tess.'

Alix went off like an anxious kitten. Tessa was so moody at times.

Tessa got up, but was perversely slow in dressing. She was angry because her dream of a little stone cottage—and its rich visitor—had been interrupted. 'Why can't we ever lead our lives as we want?' she muttered. 'Hateful school! Dull, hateful weather! And never a penny to spend!'

She could smell bacon frying downstairs, and this made her even angrier, because she knew that it was really her turn to cook. 'Alix is an interfering little fusspot!' she said.

She went slowly, grudgingly downstairs. As she went into the scullery, the back door flew open and Billy, his face red with cold, dashed in. Chip followed and flung himself at Tessa, who happened to be the nearest human being. Affectionately he banged down two muddy paws on her school dress.

'Now look what your dog has done!'

Alix was even quicker than Billy in Chip's defence. 'He didn't mean harm, Tess. I'll brush the mud off in a minute, when it's dried. It'll be all right—you'll see. But do make the tea now, Tess—please. And Billy—here's your bacon. Chris is eating his.'

In silence Tessa made the tea. Billy took his breakfast and Alix dished up the rest on to two plates, for herself and Tessa. Tessa ate quickly but Alix even more quickly, and before Tessa had finished Alix was kneeling beside her to brush off the mud of Chip's pawmarks.

So breakfast was eaten with a speed that would have horrified Aunt Elizabeth. Then the last minute rush began, as everyone left the house for school.

Soon afterwards, Mrs. Bullock came in to clean. The children were supposed to make their own beds before they went. She looked into the bedrooms. The boys' bedroom was reasonably tidy; Alix's fresh as a primrose—and the bedclothes on the bed would all have been tucked down with the most professional of hospital corners, Mrs.Bullock knew. But Tessa's room—Tessa's was in a dreadful muddle. Her bed resembled a sitting camel draped with a dustsheet. One stocking dangled from a half-open drawer. A pair of crumpled jeans and a jersey lay on the floor.

Grumbling, Mrs.Bullock remade the bed and tidied the room as best she could. 'And ten to one the girl won't even notice it.' Which was true. Tessa's eyes were too often far, far away, viewing little stone cottages and other romantic possibilities; too often she did not see the actuality under her nose. She did not want to.

That evening Tessa was preparing to go to bed in the same gloomy spirit as in the morning. The sight of an un-expectedly well-made bed and folded clothes was not go-ing to make any difference to that. But a tap on the door in-terrupted her resentful thoughts. Chris stood there, already in pyjamas and dressing gown, but with a little notebook held up in one hand—his diary. He had begun—rather importantly—to keep an engagement diary, marking down concerts he wanted to go to and making sure the dates did not clash with the meetings of the various school societies he was interested in.

But here was something quite different. 'I thought I must tell you, Tess,' he said. 'I've been looking a good way ahead at dates and—do you know, Oak-apple Day falls on a Sat-urday this year!'

'Oh, Chris! What luck!'

'Not *luck*,' Chris corrected her. 'It happens every eight years, if one Leap Year is included. If there are two, then—'

'You know what I mean,' Tessa interrupted impatiently. 'It's such a chance for us to do real justice to the birthday.'

The Stacey children always wanted to make a fuss of the double birthday, but circumstances were often against them. The date usually fell on a weekday, of course, and that meant a school day: then there was little opportunity for the elaborate preparations and celebrations which they felt would have been fitting.

This year Oak-apple Day fell on a Saturday, a school holiday. All the children would be at home; the only remaining doubt was whether their parents would be at home too. So often they had to accept professional engagements, weekdays and weekends alike.

'Supposing they are free, what should we do?' asked Tessa.

'Well, we must ask the others, of course, and discuss possibilities. We've plenty of time, after all. But what I did think—'

'Yes?'

'Well, I thought I might try to compose something in honour of the occasion that we could all play—'

'Oh, *yes*, Chris!'

Chris had often composed for organ, strings, oboe, and voice. Tessa was left out of such compositions, but she didn't mind; she had so much admiration for Chris, and thought his compositions wonderful. But this time, anyway, Chris said that he had thought of composing something for all four children to perform together for their parents.

'It sounds lovely.' But Tessa sighed. 'If only the day stays free—if only we can have it all to ourselves—just our family. If *only* it stays free. . . .'

'Well,' said Chris, 'it may.'

6

Oak-apple Day

Nearer and nearer the birthday Saturday came, and it stayed free. On the Friday morning a parcel arrived by post for Billy.

'For *me*?' He was expecting nothing; after all, it was not his birthday tomorrow.

'The handwriting is not Aunt Elizabeth's or Uncle Robert's,' said Tessa. But the postmark—' The postmark was of the village where their aunt and uncle lived.

'The person who wrote the address wasn't certain of the spelling,' observed Chris, peering.

'And whoever it was only had old brown paper and very old string to do the parcel up with,' said Alix, not without sympathy.

'Instead of more detective work,' said Mr. Stacey, 'I strongly advise opening it, to see what's inside and who sent it.'

But at that moment Billy gave an exclamation: he had suddenly realized who the sender must be, and could shrewdly guess at what had been sent. 'It's from Alf,' he said with certainty. 'He said he'd try to find some and send them in time.'

'Find what? Send what?'

'Not for you to know—yet,' said Billy to his parents. 'A secret.'

So the parcel was only opened later, in the private company of all four children. Inside the layers of tattered brown paper was an old shoe-box. Inside this, and packed carefully with protective moss, lay several twigs of oak. Among the fresh green of the oak-leaves appeared the pinky-green of galls.

'Oh!' cried Tessa and Alix with delight. 'Fancy his remembering—dear Alf!' And even sober Chris nodded in approval.

'They will look beautiful on the middle of the birthday table,' said Alix.

'In something blue,' said Tessa. 'Yes, in a Bristol Blue glass.'

'And we'll lay the table with that old, old bedspread of hand made lace,' said Alix.

'And bring out the very best dinner service that's only for special occasions.'

'And the best silver.'

'And wine glasses.'

'Only the silver will have to be cleaned first,' said Alix practically. 'And we must polish the wine glasses. Everything must sparkle for the birthday table.'

The children were determined to make this surprise a gala day; indeed, they had been planning and saving up for it for months. But for the surprise to *be* a surprise, they had to get their parents out of the way from early on Saturday morning until the evening. Mr. and Mrs. Stacey knew, of course, that their birthday would be duly celebrated, but they had no idea of the extent of the preparations. The children's surprise was to be firstly a feast, then Chris's composition. They had already been working at the music for many secret hours.

'You must give us the day to ourselves at home,' the children told their parents. 'Take sandwiches and go off somewhere for the morning and afternoon.'

'Where to?' asked Mrs. Stacey helplessly. It was so long since she and her husband had been offered the chance of such an expedition.

'Kew,' said Billy smartly; and, though they all laughed, the suggestion was adopted.

'But remember—we want you back by six, in time to change.'

'Change!' cried Mr. Stacey, who had to get into evening dress nearly every night of his life. 'Oh, must we change?'

'Of course,' said Tessa. 'Everyone must wear best clothes. Now, Alix and I will make you some sandwiches, and all you have to do is to pop off to Kew. Think of it! Everything arranged for you.'

The hearts of the Stacey parents certainly lifted. This was a rare holiday. A bit late for the first of the rhododendrons and the azaleas, but there was always something lovely at Kew. The idea had been irresistible, and when all was ready the children went to the gate to see them off.

'Six o'clock,' called Tessa. 'Not a moment before. And I shouldn't bother much about tea, because we shall be having early supper.' She did not use the word 'feast' of course. The surprise would be all the greater.

The children had saved enough money to buy a roasting chicken and a bottle of light white wine to go with it. Mrs. Bullock had bought the wine for them, after much earnest consultation. She had smuggled it in earlier in the week and it had stood in hiding behind the winter clothes in the spare room wardrobe. There were to be hot vegetables with the chicken, and Tessa planned a salad *à la Aunt Elizabeth*. Alix made herself responsible for the pudding.

As soon as their parents were safely out of the way, the

children began their preparations. Christopher went off briskly on his bicycle to collect and pay for the chicken that had been ordered. The rest started work in the kitchen : Billy chose to peel the potatoes—he laid no claim to being a cook and preferred the straightforward jobs; Tessa and Alix laid complicated plans and collected their ingredients.

The crowning glory of the feast was to be Alix's pudding. She had spent some time poring over an old cookery book and selected what seemed the most exotic dish. Among the ingredients were jelly and whipped cream and raspberries— Chris was bringing back frozen ones, when he brought the chicken. The pudding was to be made in a mould—an elaborate one with pinnacles. When it was finally turned out, it should look like a rosy, fairy castle, all edible.

While their children busied themselves, Mr. and Mrs. Stacey were sitting on the front seats of the top deck of a bus bound for Kew. The bus, like the elder Staceys, was in no hurry, and the two holiday-makers relaxed into conversation. You might have thought they would prefer to forget all family responsibilities, as well as their professional ones. In fact, they talked of their children, one by one.

Of Billy first, because they were bound for Kew and the Gardens were his kingdom. He spent as much time there as possible wandering round, often with a magnifying glass, and talking to any experts who would be talked to. And it was wonderful how many people were prepared to talk, when they realized the intense and purposeful interest in the mind of this young schoolboy.

'Billy is prepared to plod for the realization of his dreams,' said Mrs. Stacey.

'And Chris is a hard worker, too,' said Mr Stacey. 'And well liked at school, from what I gather.' They talked of Chris—of his cricket, and his mathematics, and his music, which meant so much to him, although he would not make it his career. At the moment he was particularly interested in the problems of conducting. When he went to concerts he chose the cheap seats behind the orchestra, where he could watch the conductor face to face, as it were. Tessa did not like such seats. 'All you hear is bellow from the brass,' she said. 'I don't know how you can stand it.'

Mr. Stacey quoted Tessa's remark to his wife, and added : 'There are a good many things Tessa "can't stand" but has to all the same. She feels ill-used in consequence.'

'You make her sound so disgruntled,' said Mrs. Stacey. 'But we have very happy hours together when she accompanies me. She has great musical sensibility, after all.'

'That's certainly essential in ensemble,' said Mr. Stacey. 'But it's her undoing as a soloist. She catches the spirit of the music so quickly and rarely bothers to analyze it.'

'Some people would say that fourteen is too young, anyway. . . .'

'You know that's nonsense as far as Tessa goes. I mean, in a person of such marked pianistic ability. So steeped in music, too.'

Mrs. Stacey sighed. 'I'm afraid Tessa's temperament is the difficulty.'

'Bone lazy,' said her father with sad emphasis. 'Oh, yes, she's always at the piano, but you know as well as I do that it's the quality of practice that matters. I'm afraid she's not a true artist. She's too dilatory. Besides, even if she were jolted into hard work, where would it lead? You've got to be more than good to earn a living as a concert pianist. Alix, now, could easily get into our orchestra, and she's the stuff soloists are made of.'

Mrs. Stacey made no reply immediately. She would not openly agree with her husband, but privately she did. She sighed, thinking of Alix's great musical gift, and of her determination to become a nurse instead of a professional oboist. Nursing could be not only a very hard-working way of life, but also a harrowing one. So much physical suffering to be dealt with. . . .

The Kew-bound bus was packed with people, but all were strangers, and that gave a special privacy to the Staceys' conversation. Mrs. Stacey expressed her fears for Alix. 'She is naturally so joyful, but at the same time she feels so deeply, even at this age. She can so easily be hurt. . . .'

'I don't think you need worry. She has a real toughness in her, in spite of the sensitivity. Did you notice her yesterday, leapfrogging with Billy? And when it comes to eating sausage and hash, she can beat Chris to it.'

Somehow the sausage and hash seemed very reassuring. Mrs. Stacey laughed; and the happiness of her laughter made a passenger in front turn a head to see what had amused the insignificant woman in the squashed hat.

'Kew!' shouted the conductor, and Mrs. Stacey suddenly knew that this was a memorably happy day in their lives. As they got off the bus for the Gardens, she said: 'I hope they're not working so hard at home for this evening that they're not enjoying themselves too.'

In fact the children had started their preparations so early, and with such good organization—mainly by Chris— that there was no rush or anxiety. The chicken was tucked away in the oven in good time; the vegetables and the salad would be ready at the appointed hour; and Alix's pudding—here anxiety developed unexpectedly. The moment came when she had to turn the pudding out of its mould, and realized suddenly that all depended now on the whim of the pudding and the mould—the ease with which one would consent to leave the other, the firmness with which one might continue to stand without the other. Supposing, for dreadful example, those rosy, fairy pinnacles were too soft, and collapsed?

Everyone gathered round, holding their breaths, as Alix, with scarlet cheeks and a compressed mouth, pulled at the mould that was to deliver the creation on to its special dish. There was a glugging sound, the pudding shot forth, and the next moment the astonished children beheld it underneath a kitchen chair. It was standing right side up, its pinnacles quivering indignantly, but unbroken. No one knew quite how it had happened. Alix was on the point of tears; but Chris, although speechless with laughter, resourcefully fetched a fish slicer.

'I can't look! I just can't!' cried Alix.

'Well, don't then. Now where's that dish it's supposed to be on?'

Alix shut her eyes tight. There was a tense silence, broken by Chris's heavy breathing and then a slithering sound, and the combined sighs of three people. Alix opened her eyes and beheld the pudding on its dish, on the floor, Chris lifted the dish to the dignity of the table again and dropped the fish-slice-cum-pudding-lifter into the sink.

'It was almost a pity,' said Billy, 'that Chip wasn't here. He would so have—'

But the rest of his speech was drowned by an outraged shout.

The time was near for the return of Mr. and Mrs. Stacey. The children had already laid the dining table. There was the lace bedspread, and in the centre Tessa had arranged Alf's sprays of oak-apples in their blue glass. 'Uncle Robert would have liked the effect, I'm sure,' she said. The boys had cleaned the silver and polished the glasses for the birth-day wine, and the girls had brought out the best dinner service.

They felt very satisfied as they looked round before clos-ing the dining-room door and going up to change. On the door they hung a notice saying 'No Entry' because they did not want their parents to go in until they were escorted. Besides, it was necessary to close the door because of Chip. Not that he was a thief exactly, but his head would be nearly on a level with the table, and there was no point in throwing temptation in his way. Later on, he would have some cold sausages—a favourite food of his. It was only right that he should share in the family feast.

7

'Into the Sunset'

If a feast can be crowned, the pudding crowned it.

When it appeared, Mrs. Stacey could not bear to put a spoon into such a work of art. 'It looks so beautiful. You serve it, Tessa. I don't think that Alix, as the artist, should destroy her own work.'

'Well, it was always meant to be eaten,' said Alix practically, but gratified. 'Don't forget to save some for Mrs. Bullock, Tess.' Mrs. Bullock had been much involved in the planning of the feast at every stage, and as her special contribution to the success of the evening had insisted on coming to wash up. This would allow the children to go straight on to the next part of their parents' entertainment.

The pudding was eaten in dreamy silence. It was cold and creamy. It had a tang of lemon, a taste of macaroon, as well as the freshness of the raspberries.

'That's not a pudding, it's a composition,' said Chris at last.

'But not my own,' cried Alix; and it was plain to the others what she was thinking of. Especially as she added, 'Tessa, isn't it time to go into the music room?'

'Yes. You all go in, and I'll make the coffee.'

'Coffee, too!'

'Yes, and real coffee, not instant; and the best coffee cups.

Billy washed them. They were smothered in dust, although they were in the sideboard.'

'A bit of damp and there might have been some interesting fungi,' added Billy.

In the music room the Stacey parents were seated in the most comfortable chairs. Then, when coffee was finished and the cups taken out to Mrs. Bullock in the kitchen, each received a slip of paper on which was written in capitals:

SERENADE FOR PIANO, OBOE AND STRINGS

FOR FATHER AND MOTHER

BY CHRISTOPHER STACEY.

This was a surprise indeed to Mr. and Mrs. Stacey. Father settled himself more deeply in his chair. Mother's face was in shadow, the cornflower blue of her dress spreading like the cornflower blue sky outside. The children quietly took their places, and Chris and Billy tuned their instruments. Then the others looked expectantly at Chris. 'One—and—two—and—'

The little Serenade was innocent and fresh. Mr. Stacey thought to himself that it had a strong flavour of Benjamin Britten, who was Chris's present hero. When it was over, Chris said, 'I have made an arrangement of "Billy Boy" for piano and oboe. It's a sort of jig. Would you like to hear it?'

Of course they would; and after that it was only natural that Father should get out his cello, and that Mother should sing. She sang Father's own setting of 'The Lord is my Shepherd' with cello accompaniment. Alix felt shivers down her spine and a prickling sensation in her nose. It was strange how certain sounds—a human voice, some bird voices, and her own oboe—had that effect. Tessa said that her mother's voice always made her nose run. 'It's not tears, but I get a huge drip, which is very awkward when I'm accompanying.'

It was such a happy evening. No one noticed the great cloud which had overspread the cornflower sky, until there was a crash, a silver flash of lightning, and a deluge of rain that sent Billy running to close the French windows.

Afterwards Mrs. Stacey thought that the sudden storm seemed like a forerunner of the catastrophe that was to affect them all. But at the time it seemed no more than a third surprise—a really surprising surprise to the whole family.

Rain fell for the rest of the evening, but it stopped during the night, and the next morning was clear and sunny again. The day might so easily have been an anticlimax after the excitement of the double birthday party. But in its way this Sunday was as perfect as the Saturday. They all went to church, and Mrs. Stacey sang, with Alix accompanying her on the oboe as usual. It seemed as if voice and oboe could never before have mingled so sweetly.

In the afternoon the children ran wild in the wild garden. It was hot, but with the freshness and fragrance that the rain had given the flowers. And in the evening there was sausage and hash for supper—not to be compared with roast chicken and raspberry cream pinnacles, Mrs. Stacey said apologetically; but Alix retorted that for this kind of day sausage and hash was the perfect food.

The children cooked and mashed the potatoes in the kitchen, but sizzled the sausages in a frying pan over a camp fire at the bottom of the garden. They tasted deliciously smoky. Mr. and Mrs. Stacey came down to the camp fire to eat supper with them. Billy put on an immense grey moustache from an old Christmas cracker, and pretended that he was an aged waiter and carried round the mustard.

But when he began eating his own helping of sausage and hash, he found he was eating moustache as well, so he had to take it off. Everyone laughed—it was that kind of supper-party; and Chris laughed in the middle of a mouthful and had to be beaten on the back to be saved from choking.

And then supper was over, and there was just a stack of plates to be washed, and a greasy frying pan. The sun was beginning to climb down the sky, the shadows had lengthened, and the birthday weekend was nearly over.

'A perfect two days, with perfect weather,' said Mrs. Stacey, forgetting the sudden storm of the night before. She looked round at her children and her gaze settled on Alix, a little anxiously. 'You look as if all the excitement had tired you.'

'Oh, no!' Alix was vehement. 'I could go on and on. I don't want this weekend ever to end.'

'Well, it will,' said Mr. Stacey. 'In fact, it's doing so now. Tomorrow is Monday: that means school. You should get to bed early, Alix, to be ready for it.'

'But not yet,' said Alix.

The clearing up had still to be done—this evening there was no Mrs. Bullock to take over. The children boiled a kettle of water over the remains of their camp fire, and washed up the plates and cutlery and scoured out the frying pan. Then Tessa went indoors to play some songs for her mother. Chris squatted by the glowing embers of the fire, poking them with a stick, thinking, perhaps planning. Billy, moustached again, splashed about in the stream with Chip barking at his heels.

From the house their father called softly: 'Did you ever see such a sunset? Such color!'

The others did not hear him, but Alix did. She turned her face to the western sky with eagerness, and saw the poplars, flickering gold in the evening light. She had been unwilling to let the day end tamely, and now a glorious impulse seized her. She made for the tallest poplar, crying, 'I'm going to climb. I'm going to climb higher than I've ever done before. I'll climb up and up and into the sunset. . . .'

8

Aunt Elizabeth Acts

Aunt Elizabeth and Uncle Robert sat at breakfast in what Uncle Robert called 'the sweet of the morning.' This meant that you could still see the bird's first prints, green in the dewy grass, and that the distances were blue, and the coombs or hollows in the not so distant hills filled with violet shadows. Uncle Robert said this was the reward of being early risers. He leaned back in his chair now and looked at the hills, while Aunt Elizabeth went through the letters, which had just come. They were all for her.

'Here is one from Edith,' she said, seeing Mrs. Stacey's handwriting. 'Thanking us for the birthday presents, I expect. Probably an enclosure for Alfred. Did you know he sent oak-apples for the children to decorate the table with? He and the children get on so well.'

'Dear children, those Staceys. Very dear children,' murmured Uncle Robert. 'Tessa has a good eye for grouping and color in pictures.'

'But terribly untidy.' Aunt Elizabeth slit open her sister's envelope, while Uncle Robert's mind turned to the suggestion Tessa had made when she was last with them: 'You ought to paint a picture of the well house, Uncle Robert. The lichens on the roof have such wonderful colors—gold and grey and green.' Yes, he really might paint it. With the door open, and a shaft of sunlight entering by it, and perhaps touching the figure of Alf in the dimness inside. . . .

Uncle Robert suddenly became aware of a strange silence in his wife at the other side of the breakfast table. She had read her sister's letter and sat with it in her hand, staring straight ahead of her.

'Elizabeth!' said Uncle Robert, to recall her to him. She started, and in silence handed the letter to her husband.

'*My news is so terrible*'—the letter ran—'*that I can only bear to write the bald facts. Alix fell from one of our poplar trees and is lying unconscious now in the children's hospital here. They say her life hangs in the balance. This may go on for days, weeks. I cannot bear to be away from her, but I MUST teach. I dare not give up engagements. We need the money more than ever now. I would have telephoned if you had been on the telephone; but anyway there is nothing that you could have done. . . .*'

Uncle Robert put down the letter and looked again at the bird footprints, the moving shadows on the hills. He looked at his wife, and their eyes understood each other. He went across to his desk and took out the railway timetable.

Late in the afternoon of the same day, Tessa sat in a room in the front of the Staceys' house, trying to do her prep. The boys were doing theirs at school. Mrs. Stacey was out, teaching, and Mr. Stacey was at the hospital with Alix.

Tessa read the same paragraph in her geography book five times and knew no more about it than when she had read it the first time. Her head ached abominably, and the room in which she sat was stifling and smelt faintly of breakfast. The windows were closed, but Tessa could not be bothered to get up and open them. A fly walked, buzzing, up a pane, slipped back to the bottom, and began his ineffectual walk again. And again; and again.

'Oh, the idiotic creature!' cried Tessa at last. She crossed the room and flung up the window. The fly escaped, and Tessa leaned her arms on the sill. She wondered wearily what to do about supper. Mrs. Bullock had left a note saying that there was cold meat and that she had peeled some potatoes. Mrs. Bullock, in her noisy distress at the news of Alix's accident, had said over and over again that they must all eat and that she would see that they did not forget to do so. But the very thought of food sickened Tessa now.

A car drew up. The hedge hid its occupants from Tessa, but after a moment she saw the iron gate pushed open and a tall figure with a basket in one hand, an elegantly rolled umbrella in the other, walk up the path, the long feet turned slightly outward. Following came the taxi driver, carrying a suitcase.

'Aunt Elizabeth!'

Seeing the suitcase, Tessa's mind flew to the spare room. The wardrobe was full of mother's concert dresses and everyone's winter coats. There were football boots up there, and hockey sticks. Piles of old music lay upon the bed—Tessa groaned.

She went and opened the front door, Chip following. He gave a self-deprecatory wag of the tail, and Tessa smiled tremulously. Aunt Elizabeth gazed down at her for a moment, then pointed with her umbrella at the suitcase. 'In the hall, please.' The taxi driver dumped it, received his money, and went off.

'The basket of produce had better go into the kitchen, Tessa. Everything in it is fresh from the garden, but it should be unpacked.'

Tessa picked up the basket and stood uncertainly. She couldn't leave Aunt Elizabeth in the hall. 'Won't you come into the music room? And can I make you some tea?'

'Thank you, no. Your parents are out, I suppose?'

Tessa explained where everyone was, and her aunt said, 'On second thoughts, leave the basket. Instead, carry my suitcase upstairs and show me the spare bedroom.'

'It's in a dreadful muddle, Aunt Elizabeth.'

'I've dealt with muddles before now.' Aunt Elizabeth went upstairs, Tessa following, like a tug escorting a great liner into dock. Tessa opened the spare room door and hesitated. Then bravely she put the suitcase on to the bed, making a space for it by pushing aside the pile of music. She looked at her aunt in a kind of despair. Her head was hammering; she thought she might have to be sick.

Aunt Elizabeth opened her suitcase and took out a nylon coverall and a bottle of aspirin. 'You go to bed, Tessa, and get rid of that headache. I'll bring you some aspirin with water presently.'

As Tessa crept between the sheets, she wondered how Aunt Elizabeth had guessed about the headache. It did not occur to her that Aunt Elizabeth herself had once been subject to these blinding attacks. So far Alix had been the only one who really understood. At this thought Tessa's eyes filled with tears, but she knew that this time they were for herself and not for Alix. She brushed them angrily away.

Aunt Elizabeth came in with the aspirin and a tumbler of water. She pulled the curtains across the windows, filling the room with cool green shade. Tessa's last waking thought was: 'I wonder how she's getting on with the spare room? Poor old thing!'

Aunt Elizabeth felt herself to be a good many things, but

never a poor old one. Now, with an expression of determined hauteur, she put on the nylon coverall and set about
making the spare room habitable. She piled all the music
on the top of the cupboard and put the football boots
tidily at the bottom. The hockey sticks she propped in a
corner.

In the linen cupboard she found clean sheets and pillow-
cases. She saw with thankfulness that there was a bulb in the
table lamp, and that it worked. She found a duster and a
mop : she dusted the tops of the furniture—a slovenly way
of cleaning, of which she disapproved, but there must be
so much to be done, outside this room. She mopped the
linoleum and shook the bedside mat vigorously from the
window. There were two large empty drawers in the chest,
and into these she placed her meticulously folded clothes
and found room in the wardrobe for her dresses.

She washed and creamed her hands, took up a pair of
rubber gloves, and went downstairs. Picking up the basket
of vegetables from the hall floor, she went into the kitchen
and began to make a salad for supper.

The boys felt a kind of relief when they arrived back
and saw Aunt Elizabeth in charge. It was the sort of relief
you might feel if a very efficient Gorgon came to keep house
for you; so long as you did nothing to bring on that stare
of disapproval, you were all right. So said Chris.

Mr. Stacey did not come home for supper. He had to go
straight from the hospital to a church choir practice. Mrs.
Stacey appeared, however, white faced and tired. She had
managed to meet her husband on his way from the hospital
and get his news of Alix; but there was no news. She had
still not recovered consciousness. Her condition was critical.

Mrs. Stacey ate a little of the supper prepared for them,
but she seemed abstracted. She listened always for the

telephone. The hospital would ring if there was the slightest indication of any change in Alix.

Later, when the boys had gone to bed, the two sisters sat in the music room. Big brown moths fluttered round the lamp. The evening primroses spread themselves and shone palely in the dusk. Against the sky stood the tall poplar from which Alix had fallen, so short a time ago.

At first they sat in silence, and then they began to talk, mostly of Alix. Staring at the tree and thinking of Alix—almost hearing that delighted laughter—Aunt Elizabeth felt a pain at her heart that made her exclaim waspishly: 'Those children have been allowed to run wild! They are quite undisciplined! Such an accident should never have been allowed to happen!'

Two spots of colour burned suddenly in Mrs. Stacey's pale cheeks. 'How dare you say so, Elizabeth! They have always had a great deal of freedom, it's true, but that has taught them responsibility. They are reliable children—you have said so yourself.' Aunt Elizabeth nodded. 'Such an accident could have happened to any lively child.' Mrs. Stacey's voice became quiet. Her anger had died. She would not, she *could* not feel anger while Alix lay so white and still. While Alix lay so desperately out of the reach of the love of her mother and of all her family.

Mrs. Stacey looked across at her sister and saw from her face in the dusk that she was feeling something of the same restraint. Yet Aunt Elizabeth had reproached her for risks wantonly taken. And then, with one of those sudden, strange quirks of the mind which come even in the midst of deepest anxiety, a flash of memory brought a vivid picture to Mrs. Stacey. It seemed more real than the quiet shadowy room in which they sat. She looked at the regal figure opposite, but saw instead the Elizabeth of years and years ago, of their childhood together. This Elizabeth was dressed in an old cotton frock stained with the greens and browns of tree climbing. She was swinging her long black-stockinged legs, sitting high, very high in the branches of a tall elm. She was drinking cold cocoa from a medicine bottle. Between gulps she was shouting to the young Edith—now Edith Stacey, the singer—to 'come on up! I dare you!'

9

The Shadow of a Smile

Alix still lay unconscious.

One of her family was always with her, if possible, keeping vigil by the bedside. All the family came in turn, with the exception of Aunt Elizabeth and Billy.

Aunt Elizabeth said that she wouldn't go, because others had prior claim; and that was that. Billy went once, at his special request, but came away so white, silent, and strained-looking that his mother said he should not go again, and Aunt Elizabeth backed up the decision. Billy himself did not demur.

The one who spent most time with Alix was Tessa; she spent every free hour at the hospital. Tessa felt somehow that Alix—even Alix unconscious—needed her; and she knew that she needed Alix. So she was glad to leave the ordinary, breathless bustle of everyday life for the echoing corridors and quiet, quick figures in white coats, white caps, and white aprons. Then to open the door of the side ward and enter a quiet world within a world. Here Alix lay.

From outside Alix's room, muffled, came continuous sounds of hospital activity. Quick feet; the rattle of crockery; the slow, thumping tread of ambulance men; voices—often softer or sharper than English, for many of the hospital staff were foreign.

Inside the room, stillness, sunlight quivering on a bowl

63

of roses. Alix lay quietly, and Tessa sat watching her, longing for some movement, however slight, that might mean
the return of consciousness.

In these hours Tessa felt herself nearer to Alix than she
had ever been before. She seemed to understand her. The
very surroundings—the quiet, the order, and the coming
and going of the nurses—carried her into Alix's hopes.
Alix had wanted to be a hospital nurse, but now—now—

To be a nurse. . . .

The nurses who came into the side ward sometimes
stopped for a few moments to talk. One was a West Indian,
always gay, yet gentle and quiet when she came to attend
to Alix. Tessa watched her deftness and marvelled at the
knowledge and skill and patience that must lie behind it.

Tessa watched so intently that the little nurse noticed
it.

'You want to be a nurse some day?' she asked.

'Oh, *no*,' said Tessa startled. 'I'm going to be—I'm going to be—' She stopped. She had suddenly realized with
certainty that she was *not* going to be a professional
musician. That had been a dream—less than a dream. She
did not even regret its passing. But what, then, was she
going to be?

'Going to be—going to be—' The little West Indian nurse
mimicked her, gently rallying. 'She doesn't know what she's
going to be.'

'My sister—my sister there, she wanted to be a nurse,'
said Tessa.

The West Indian was silent for a moment, then said
quietly: 'A nurse—it's a very good thing to want to be. I
have a little sister, and I say to her, you could be a nurse
too. We *need* nurses. All the world needs nurses. If you
are right for a nurse, you should *be* a nurse.'

'There's a lot of hard work, isn't there?' said Tessa. 'And dull too, sometimes?'

'Everything good has some of that,' said the little nurse briskly. 'Nobody to be afraid of that, please.' She looked into Tessa's eyes as she moved to the door.'*You* are not afraid of that, you know. Not really.' She went out, leaving Tessa staring after her.

In other brief conversations Tessa gradually learnt a good deal about the nurses' lives—of the long hours of work, the periods off for 'school' when they studied for exams, the night duty in the great dim wards.

Many thoughts which had never before entered Tessa's mind now filled it. And dreamy, muddled Tessa began to face them squarely.

She began to talk of her changing ideas to Christopher. He had just come from a visit to the hospital ('No. No change.') and gone down to the stream at the bottom of the garden, by the fateful poplars. There Tessa found him. They sat in silence for a while. Neither spoke of Alix; both were thinking of her.

Then Tessa said, 'I think I'm giving up the idea of music, after all—I mean, as a career.'

Chris simply said, 'Yes, Tessa.' He had always known she ought to do this. The decision was one that—for himself—he had come to regretfully, but soberly, some time ago.

'Yes, Tessa,' said Christopher again, and put an arm round her shoulders. She cried a little, not for herself, but for the blackbird voice of Alix's oboe that was silent now, and for the trim hospital nurses that went around Alix's bed and whose number Alix might never now join.

Tessa's new found perception did not extend much beyond Alix and herself, and only one person—apart from

Chip—had time to notice the mute, continuing misery of Billy. And that person was Aunt Elizabeth.

Everyone had felt relief at the coming of Aunt Elizabeth. The feeling of relief persisted, although now taken for granted. Perhaps only Mrs. Bullock still really noticed. She had at first been suspicious of the intruder; soon, rather unwillingly, an admirer. 'Her High and Mightiness certainly knows her onions,' she confided to Mr. Bullock. 'Shop! She really gets her money's worth of shopping. She's choosy. She never brings in a vegetable that doesn't look fresh from the soil. One day she says to me—"What about a steak pie, Mrs. Bullock?" I tells her the family haven't had a steak pie in years. "Then it's about time they did," says she. And off come her rings and up go her sleeves, and she makes a pie that would put shame to a Lord Mayor's Banquet. And the mending and the darning that little Alix used to do— not a potato in a sock to be seen! You can hardly see the darns at all, for that matter.'

Aunt Elizabeth cared for the Staceys' food and for their clothing, and now—certainly as far as Billy went—for much more. One day she had seen in a shop window a poster giving details of gardens which were thrown open to the public. She chose one that she judged to be within a reasonable bus ride of the Stacey home.

On the Friday evening of that week Billy went into the kitchen to find Aunt Elizabeth making sausage-rolls. 'Some of these are for us, Billy. Tomorrow you and I are going to Hornhurst Gardens. I'm a bit of a botanist myself, and we'll see who can find the most unusual plants.'

Billy's face lit up. 'What about Chip?' He watched Aunt Elizabeth's expression anxiously: would a cat lover agree to taking a dog on such an expedition? Yet without Chip the expedition would lose half its charm for Billy.

'He'd have to be on a lead,' said Aunt Elizabeth. 'Would he mind?'

'I think he'd rather be on a lead, and come.'

So they went off the next morning with Chip on the floor of the bus between Billy's knees. The journey passed in easy conversation. Aunt Elizabeth asked about Chip's curious name, and Billy told her the story of the old block. Then, after a hesitation, he spoke of Alix's longing for a dog. 'I've tried to share Chip with her, but he won't really be shared. He likes everyone—I think he'd even like a burglar, but he's miserable without me.'

They made an incongruous trio: Aunt Elizabeth, splendidly hatted as usual, a truly imposing figure; Billy, thin and leggy, his coat sleeves too short to conceal his long wrists; Chip, too shaggy for a labrador, too tall for a bassett hound, mournful-eyed. Clearly he didn't feel mournful, however, in spite of the lead. The three began to spend a quietly happy day together.

A great part of the gardens sloped to a valley in which lay a lake. This part had, in fact, been planted with care, but it appeared to be almost wild. There was one beech tree, standing alone, which Billy said was worth coming miles to see. They sat on a bench on the terraced slope, looking at the profusion of trees; at the mingling of colors —pale gold, purple, bronze, burning red, and greens from lime color to almost black.

In the formal gardens they had found roses, their petals like velvet or satin or stiff silk. They were the roses of Aunt Elizabeth's hats, but with the delicacy of life.

'Have you a favourite flower?' Billy asked. He expected her to plump for roses.

'No. Roses *are* lovely! But I can think of wild flowers that I love, too—harebells and celandine and white

wind-flowers; primroses and an old thorn-tree in bloom:
I'm thankful I was brought up in the country.'

'You always look as if you had been brought up in Marble
Halls!' Billy felt bold to have made this sally.

The dimple appeared in Aunt Elizabeth's cheek. 'My
Marble Halls were the same as your mother's, you know,
Billy. They were farmhouse walls, rough and thick. Always
there seemed to be the smell of bread baking, and hay,
and leather. And the wind in the elms blowing the rooks
like burnt paper across the sky. Your mother and I used
to watch them. . . .'

'Sisters can be different,' Billy said thoughtfully. 'I suppose Alix and Tessa are very different. Alix. . . .'

The idea of Alix was never far from his mind nowadays,
although he could seldom bring himself to speak of her.
To speak of her on the bus that morning—to tell Aunt
Elizabeth of her longing for a dog—had been a measure-
less relief to Billy.

Now he said slowly, 'I wish that Alix—I *wish* that
Alix—'

He could say no more. Aunt Elizabeth nodded in under-
standing, so vehemently it seemed that the roses in her
hat must shed at least one petal. Then they sat in stillness
again, and in silence.

At that moment Mr. and Mrs. Stacey sat in the same
kind of silence, alone together in a railway carriage, coming
away from a cathedral town north of London. Mrs. Stacey
had been singing in the cathedral, to her husband's cello
accompaniment, 'The Lord is my Shepherd. I shall not
want. . . .' Thinking of Alix, she had almost broken down,
but the artist in her rose and forbade this. She had gone on
to the end: 'In the valley of the shadow of death I will
fear no evil. . . .'

She was thinking of this again, and in the privacy of the railway carriage Mr. Stacey took her hand. They talked, of Alix and of those things that had to do with Alix : of Aunt Elizabeth's kindness; of Tessa's giving up all her free time for the hospital; of Chris's stalwartness in this time of trouble; of Billy's avid listening to any scrap of news after the hospital visit.

This evening Mr. and Mrs. Stacey had arranged to go directly to the hospital from the station. The staff allowed the family to see Alix whenever they could, so tonight the two of them slipped in without troubling anyone.

Tessa was sitting by the bed, Alix's hand in hers. A green-shaded lamp burned in a bracket on the wall, but it was hardly necessary, as the room was still pearly with light from the long June evening.

Tessa did not turn her head at the sound of an entry. She was gazing intently at Alix.

As her parents approached the bed, Alix's eyelids flickered, opened.

'Look !' breathed Tessa, her face transfigured.

Alix looked at her mother, and there was recognition in the look. A shadow of a smile, then her eyes closed again, this time to a gentle sleep.

10

Nightmare

At first, to the Stacey children, Alix's return to consciousness seemed like a happy-ever-after ending. Their parents were more subdued in their rejoicing. They knew that the hospital staff still felt anxiety, and they feared for the future.

After the first recognition of her mother Alix slept a great deal. Waking, she was too weak to wonder at her surroundings—why she was here in bed, in a hospital. For at first she remembered nothing.

Then came a terrible moment of returning memory. She remembered her fall. She remembered falling, and then it seemed she was always falling; her dreams became haunted. In her dreams she ran along roads which suddenly narrowed into ledges high on a towering wall of rock. Sometimes a black chasm would open before her. Sometimes she seemed to be clinging with her fingertips to a massive rock-face dreadful to look up to, and dropping away to depths beyond thought. Sometimes she was leaning further and further over a low wall, staring into bottomless depths, drawn irresistibly into danger.

From all these dreams Alix woke in terror, soaking with sweat, exhausted. Sometimes she shook so violently that her teeth chattered.

It seemed almost as nightmarish to be awake as to be

asleep. The doctors and nurses were kind, but their kindness could not reassure her. Everything seemed strange and more than life-size, confusing and terrifying.

This was the first time Alix had ever been torn from the safe circle of her family. Her parents saw her as often as they could, and she clung to them, but almost hopelessly. The boys came, but these visits seemed to excite her so much that the head nurse thought it better on the whole if her brothers stayed away. Tessa came without fail, but not even to Tessa could Alix really unburden herself.

Alix's first efforts at sitting up had brought on nausea and giddiness, but gradually she was becoming stronger. To an outsider she seemed to be making reasonably good progress. She was quiet, obedient, and co-operative; but those in charge worried about her. Too quiet, they said; too withdrawn.

Then, one morning, the strange thing happened. Sound ceased for Alix. The sudden silence seemed like the muffling of snowfall. Almost as though it had been snowing *inside* the hospital, so that the wards and passages were covered with it and even people's footsteps were soundless.

The coming of this new and eerie silence was one more thing to frighten her when it happened. Alix tried to forget her fears by reading. She was reading when the doctors came into the room and spoke to her. She did not raise her head from her book; she had not heard them.

Alix had become deaf.

The new development seemed to puzzle the doctors. They could only suppose, they said, that this was a very rare condition resulting from severe nervous strain. They made various tests and examinations. As a result they offered the comfort that, at least, Alix's deafness was not due to any brain injury. She *might* recover. And apart from the deafness, anyway, a slow but sure physical recovery could be hoped for. . . . The deafness itself was another matter.

The news of Alix's deafness had dazed the Staceys at first. Then the shattered family rallied and united in the one thought—what was best for Alix?

Chris was the most prompt and practical in his ideas. Handicapped by total deafness, Alix might have to be looked after not only now but for many years to come, and provision would have to be made for her. Chris said that he had been told at school that there was a good possibility of his winning a math scholarship to a University. 'That would mean a longer time before I actually started earning,' he said, 'but I'd probably get a better job in the end. A job with better pay—that will be important.'

'And I want to qualify as a nurse,' said Tessa. They all stared. 'I haven't told you this before, but I've really thought it out. I'll do nursing. If I did private or district nursing after I'd qualified, then I could have a home to offer Alix. I mean, when the time came for father to want to retire.'

Aunt Elizabeth, who was now part of the family circle, had listened with admiration to Christopher, and with admiration and amazement to Tessa. And now she observed Billy, the last of the three Stacey children, and his silence spoke as clearly to her as their words. Billy was silent because he felt useless. If he became the kind of botanist he hoped, he might well have to spend his time wandering all over the world in search of his plants. And how would that help Alix?

How could Billy ever help Alix? Aunt Elizabeth, guessing his thought, laid a hand over his in reassurance.

Mr. and Mrs. Stacey remained silent too. The surge of

family unity and feeling, and the directness and common-sense of the two elder children almost overwhelmed them. Their feelings were too strong for words.

Aunt Elizabeth, without withdrawing her hand from Billy's, broke the silence with an observation of great sense : 'We must not forget,' she said, 'that Alix may be capable, after all, of earning her own living in time. Certainly she will want to do so, if she possibly can. Not nursing now, of course; not music. But she is, for example, already an excellent needlewoman. She might be able to do something with that. She might start by attending classes in dress-making and dress-designing. There are several possible openings for someone of Alix's abilities and character, even now. She will want to try planning some future of her own, as soon as she begins to feel well again.'

' Aunt Elizabeth went on to declare her intention of stopping with the family until Alix was at least convalescent. She suggested that later on Alix might benefit from a holiday with her and Uncle Robert.

This led to another question—would Alix return to school that term?

Mrs. Stacey said quietly, 'The real problem is, will Alix ever be able to return to her old school; or will she have to attend some kind of special school?'

The children stared at their mother, appalled. Her words brought home to them more fully the meaning of Alix's tragedy. . . . Then, strangely, each began to concentrate on something which had nothing to do with their present problems.

Chris noticed how a tree in the garden opposite swayed in the wind, so that it resembled a great green beast, nodding and gaping.

Billy watched Mr. Baker pass the gate and noticed that

his bitch, Bella, was swaying and round as a barrel with the puppies she was soon to have.

Tessa stared at the carpet—they were in the dining-room—seeing, as though she had never seen them before, the threadbare patches made by the feet of the family as they sat at meals.

Mr. Stacey spoke at last. 'Alix's present and future is something very difficult for us even to begin to imagine as yet. We must be patient. We must find ways and means, as we see what the possibilities are. We must be determined and we must also be patient. For Alix's sake.'

Later that night, in bed, Chris turned and tossed, his mind full of schemes. Billy had taken Chip to bed—not really allowed—and wept into his fur. Aunt Elizabeth sat at her dressing table and thought of the small amount of capital she had invested. 'It might come in useful for Alix, later. I must consult Robert.'

And Tessa went to bed, but could not sleep, and rose before sunrise. She crept out of bed to the dormer window of her bedroom and looked down the length of the garden, to where the poplar leaves gleamed silvery in the translucent summer night.

She realized that night was already beginning to melt into day. Soon she would hear the first birds. She remembered Alix, shining-eyed, telling her of the dawn chorus that she and Billy had heard, in Alf's company.

The little stream at the bottom of the garden gurgled and plopped. All at once a blackbird sang softly. Tessa, listening, thought of Alix's oboe. She laid her head down upon her folded arms in a gesture of mourning.

I I

The Homecoming

Alix's deafness removed her even further into a world of her own. Her eyes searched faces for the meaning of what she could not hear; she watched moving lips eagerly, but lip reading is not quickly to be learnt. She often had to ask her visitors to write down what they wanted to say, and then stared disappointedly at the words scrawled on the paper.

She never complained, but she could not eat or sleep properly, and had no taste now for reading. She seemed to live only for her visitors, and yet the visits left her sad and unsatisfied. Once Mrs.Stacey said anxiously to Tessa: 'You haven't told Alix that you want to be a nurse?'

'No, not yet. But why?'

'Because—well, it might hurt her, as well as please her. After all, *she* had decided to be a nurse.'

Tessa said, 'I know what you mean, Mother. But I have a feeling—I'm sure, in fact—that's not what she'd most regret now.'

'What then?'

'Her oboe.'

Mrs.Stacey turned her head to hide the tears that fell. Then she controlled herself and turned back to Tessa: 'Yes, perhaps that's true. Perhaps one cannot fully realize the delight and blessing of sound until one has been deprived of it. A harsh saying.'

Tessa nodded. Her mother went on: 'You have a new wisdom, Tessa. And you have a new commonsense and help-fulness for which your father and I are grateful—*so* grate-ful. You are a support to the whole family now, and that means a support to Alix.'

Tessa flushed. No more was said.

It became apparent that as soon as Alix was able, she would be better at home. She was progressing too slowly in hospital. The doctor said that as well as good food she needed fresh air, interests, and cheerfulness round her, to build up her strength. These she should get at home.

So, in a week or ten days, Alix was to come home. Even before this was finally decided, Chris had started on one of his schemes. He took out some of his savings and went to Mr. Baker's timber yard. He had a long and mysterious con-versation with Mr. Baker which ended in a delivery of timber in the Staceys' garden.

Then Chris started work, and Billy—having been let into the secret—joined him. Mr. Baker too, often seemed to be 'happening to pass' and would join them—providing tools, giving advice, and often lending a hand himself. Between them they were building a hut at the bottom of the Stacey's garden—a little log-cabin, with one of its four sides open to the air, so that Alix could rest there and freely look out.

'Do you think she'll mind being near the poplars?'

'Of course not. Her fall wasn't the poplar's fault, and she'll love being near the stream.'

The cabin was finished the evening before Alix was due to come out of hospital. As Mr. Baker helped to put the finishing touches to the structure, he told the boys that Bella had just had her pups: 'Jack Russells this time, by the look of them.'

So Billy, with Chip, went back with Mr. Baker to see the

new family. Bella was indoors having her supper at the time, or there might have been trouble.

Chip sniffed at the little crawling creatures. This was perhaps the first time he had seen such young puppies. He had met Bella's litters before, but when they had already grown into boisterous youngsters. Then he had suffered himself to be walked over, to have his ears used as a teeth-ing rubber, his tail sat on. He had even been growled at with tiny growls which—so Billy insisted—had made him grin. In fact, Chip was as easy-going with other dogs as with human beings.

Observing this, Mr. Baker had once said, 'If you ever had a second dog, you'd have no trouble from Chip.' And now he said: 'You could have one of this new litter as a gift, if you liked.'

'A second dog?' said Billy. 'But—'

'I know, I know. Plenty of arguments against it. But a puppy playing about round that little cabin would be a pretty thing, a cheerful thing.'

'For Alix. . . .' Billy said slowly. 'I see what you mean.'

'Plenty of time, anyway. Too young to leave their mother for a while yet. Let me know later. . . .'

Billy came thoughtfully away from Mr. Baker's: perhaps this was going to be something he could do to help Alix in the near future.

The next day, in the morning, Alix came home. The ex-citement exhausted her, but in the afternoon she had re-covered enough to be taken down the garden to see her log-cabin.

Aunt Elizabeth had put a camp-bed into it; she had also made a mattress from foam rubber and covered it with gay material. Tessa had used some of the same material to cover two cushions. There were bookshelves with favourite books already on them.

'It's—it's a dear little house,' said Alix softly. In the old days she would have cried out for joy; now, not hearing her own voice, she seldom raised it. 'A dear little house,' Alix repeated. 'I'll be able to lie here and see the sky and the stream. There are dragonflies too; and I remember, birds come to drink and bathe. Oh, it's wonderful, wonderful! Thank you.'

I2

Sammy

Alix's joy in being home again did all that the doctors had hoped for. Her appetite returned, and Aunt Elizabeth and Mrs. Bullock saw to it that there was good food to satisfy it. Her thin cheeks began to fill out; the long hours she spent in the cabin freshened and browned her skin and made her sleep well at nights.

Although she still had to rest a great deal, she was gradually regaining physical strength. Aunt Elizabeth, remembering the old Alix, brought her socks to be darned; and she interested Alix in making herself a summer frock.

Tessa borrowed books from the public library, studying Alix's tastes, and took them to the little cabin. Alix read a great deal now, and Tessa persuaded her to do some of her reading aloud. She read to Tessa, gaining confidence again in her own voice, which she never heard now. She would hesitate over an unfamiliar word or perhaps mispronounce one. Then Tessa stopped her, and rounded or stretched her own lips to the correct sound. Alix watched earnestly and tried to repeat the sound, until Tessa signalled that the difficulty was overcome.

Alix was not going to remain an invalid. Gradually she fell into her old ways of doing little necessary jobs about the house; gradually, too, the other chidren became more accustomed to her disability. In one way Alix was glad:

she had never wanted to be treated differently from anyone else. In another way, she was sometimes frightened. She realized that whatever happens, life goes on—and that it is better, at whatever cost, to make oneself part of it. There were hurdles that no one else could climb for you; things you had to suffer or overcome alone.

She had moments of depression, especially in the hours before sunrise, empty of bird song for her. Then there seemed to be nothing but greyness. But, if the worst came to the worst, she could always rap on the walls and her mother would come to her. 'Just so that you remember that you are not alone,' her mother said, and Alix was comforted. All the kindness in the world could not solve her problems for her, but it could give her strength towards solving them for herself.

The oboe had been put away in Mrs. Stacey's room, and Alix did not ask for it. She never saw the family gathered together for the usual rehearsals, and she made no inquiry. But one evening, coming downstairs for a glass of water, she discovered that they always waited until she had gone to bed. Then they began rehearsing, knowing she could not hear them.

they should practice whenever it was most convenient for they should practice whenever it was most convenient for them.

She thought she had put music out of her mind, but now it returned to haunt her, like a ghost. She began to hear music in her dreams. She studied the scores of the oratorios she knew so well, and heard them in her mind. Yet the ghost-music was worse than no music. She seemed to lose all heart and became listless. Mrs. Stacey thought that she was losing weight again, and Aunt Elizabeth agreed. The two elder children were too busy with school exams to notice the change, but Billy did, and he knew that this was his great opportunity. He went to his father.

'Father, Alix has to spend so much time alone. Do let her have one of Mr. Baker's puppies. They're just old enough to leave their mother now.' Mr. Stacey was taken aback by the revival of the old suggestion. 'Do, do, *do*, father. They're Jack Russells this time and shouldn't grow very big. Please, father. Just for Alix's sake!'

Mr. Stacey considered carefully. 'What about Chip?'

'Oh, he won't mind. He's seen the puppies already.'

'Then, there is training. Could Alix manage that?'

'Of course she can. The puppy would soon get used to her voice, and she can have one of those dog whistles that only dogs can hear. *Please*, Father. She needs someone jolly to play with.'

'Ye-s. That's true, certainly. I believe you have more sense than the lot of us, Bill. All right.'

Billy rushed straight off to tell Mr. Baker, who slapped his knee and laughed aloud with satisfaction. Then home again, secretly to prepare a comfortable bed for the puppy. Billy sawed three sides of a wooden box down to about six inches, and one side down almost to nothing. Then he put in an old cushion and a piece of blanket. He bought a dog whistle from the pet shop. He very much wanted to buy a collar and a lead, too, but felt that Alix would like to get these herself.

Now, when all preparations were made, he could break the news to Alix. When he approached the log cabin, Alix saw his face alight with excitement and pleasure. He seized a piece of paper, and wrote—'A surprise for you! Come and get it. More fun if you shut your eyes. Let me lead you.'

Full of wonder, Alix agreed. She even submitted to being turned round and round in the street several times, so that she did not know in which direction she was facing. Then, with her eyes squeezed honorably tight, she put her hand into Billy's and went off to her unknown destination.

It wasn't really very far, but it seemed a long time to Alix before they came to a halt. They had gone through a door or a gate, and yet she was sure they were still in the open. Something warm and soft tumbled over her feet, as Billy said triumphantly, 'Now open your eyes!' She found herself in a wire netting enclosure, in one corner of which was a shed. Mr. Baker stood to one side, beaming at them.

The enclosure seemed full of puppies—there were, in fact, only five—so exuberant were they. Chasing gnats, if there were any; if not, just chasing. Trying out a tug-o'-war with a much chewed rubber ring; making a rugger scrum over an old ball. The clown of the family was the smallest. He was white, with pricked brown ears. He had a rakish expression due to a brown patch over one eye, which made him look as though he had recently engaged in a brawl; and he had a minute brown tail which stood bolt upright.

He was quicker than his brothers and sisters, snatching the ball or the ring from their very jaws. When he saw Alix he made a dash at her, and tried to scramble up her legs. She crouched and picked him up, and immediately his bones seemed to melt and he lay, soft and warm and smelling of hay, against her neck. After a moment he scrabbled down her back, and fell head over heels in his anxiety to see what had been going on among the others during his brief absence.

When Alix realized that one of the puppies was for her, the choice was already made. For her it must be the one who had lain against her neck, and who was, she was sure, the gayest, the most gallant, the nimblest of them all.

Mr. Baker lent the children a basket with a lid, and together they bore the puppy home.

Chip took the arrival very well. He gazed anxiously into Billy's face, but soon understood that this was Alix's dog; he need fear no rival. The following morning, early, when Alix went down to the kitchen, she found the puppy—whom she had already named Sammy—fast asleep in the very center of Chip's bed. Chip himself was curled patiently round the edge.

Now, there began for Alix a new life. Every morning before breakfast she and Sammy went out, sometimes with Billy and Chip, sometimes alone. At first she had been nervous, but Sammy forced her to overcome that. She took sensible precautions. Since she could not hear approaching traffic, she was particularly careful crossing the roads. On a road without a pavement she always walked well to the right, to face oncoming cars.

The Staceys lived on the edge of the Green Belt—in their part, some miles of heathland, dotted with gorse and old thorn. All kinds of grasses grew there, and it was a favorite place in summer for larks, yellow-hammers, and goldfinches. Here Alix and Sammy roved often.

Alix bought a collar and a lead for Sammy on her first shopping expedition since her fall. Sammy learnt to tolerate these—as a puppy, he had so much to learn, and Alix was a patient teacher. Once they were on the heath, Alix exchanged the lead for a very long piece of cord, to give Sammy greater freedom. Then, when at last Sammy had been trained to understand and obey the summons of the dog whistle, she let him free altogether. He fancied himself as a butterfly hunter careering after brown tortoiseshells or common blues, but never catching anything.

And so, part of Alix's great burden of loneliness—the

inevitable loneliness of silence—was lifted. It was impossible not to feel the gulf which separated her from her family, however much both sides tried to bridge it with their love; but no such gulf existed between her and this rampantly cheerful little animal who rollicked up at her call. Sammy could play hide and seek, or hunt-the-ball, and was a great one for a joke. The rest of the family often heard them outside together—Sammy growling or barking with mock ferocity; Alix laughing as she had not laughed since that weekend of Oak-apple Day. Then the two would come indoors together: Alix would plump down, rosy-cheeked and panting, and Sammy would scramble into her lap. There he lay, paws dangling, and would promptly fall asleep, like the trustful baby he was.

13

Alf Sees for Himself

What kind of school Alix could attend was still not clear. In the meantime, at least she could begin schoolwork again on her own—a little every day. Chris set her sums; Tessa, history and geography. Mr. and Mrs. Stacey sometimes smiled together at Tessa's new seriousness in her own school subjects; but they had faith in it, too.

Alix continued reading aloud, and she began to study botany with Billy. He showed her how to identify the different grasses they found on the heath, and many hidden small flowers.

The time had come when Aunt Elizabeth felt she ought to leave the Staceys. The worst of their crisis was over; and the more Alix could take on her old household responsibilities, the better for her. That was to be part of the treatment the hospital recommended. Besides, Uncle Robert had been a very long time alone.

So Aunt Elizabeth was going home, and she suggested that Alix should go back with her for a short time.

'And Sammy?' said Alix doubtfully, when the plan was explained to her.

'He's housetrained,' said Aunt Elizabeth, 'and I've seen how careful you are to wipe his paws, and I know you will not let him annoy Captain McIvor. Yes, we invite Sammy too.'

Alix still stared at her anxiously, not sure of what her aunt had ben saying, although the expression on her face had been favorable. To make things quite clear Aunt Elizabeth nodded her head.

'You mean Sammy *can* come, too?'

Aunt Elizabeth was so emphatic that she seemed in danger of nodding her head off; and Alix laughed aloud with pleasure.

When the time came for them actually to go, however, Alix felt sudden fear. Bustle and noise can be bewildering, but bustle and *silence* terrifying. At the railway station Sammy was nervous too—of the crowds hurrying this way and that, of the thundering trains, and of the loaded luggage trucks. His whole body trembled in Alix's arms. Alix clasped him to her, and in comforting him she forgot her own fear. Aunt Elizabeth, who had been shepherding Alix along, observed the change with satisfaction.

The rail journey was not a long one, and at the end, Uncle Robert was waiting for them with his elderly but very sprucely kept car. Aunt Elizabeth went pink with pleasure at the sight of him waiting on the platform; and he beamed back like a cheerful sun. Then he turned to Alix and caught her, Sammy and all, in a warm embrace. Over her head his face lost some of its brightness, as Aunt Elizabeth saw; but he resumed his cheerful manner as they went together towards the car.

Driving home, Alix exclaimed at the views of the downs, although she had seen them so often. Uncle Robert stopped the car on a rise so that they could let their eyes dwell on the long, lovely line against the sky. He made Alix understand that here was one of the places where they could go for walks. They would take picnic lunches, and Sammy would have the time of his life on the springy turf of the downs.

When they reached the house, Alf was waiting for them, to take their cases and to see Alix for himself. He had been told of her affliction, but had been absolutely unable to believe it.

'You mean to say she can't hear her own little pipe any more?' he had asked Uncle Robert incredulously.

'She doesn't even play it any more, Alf.'

Alf had glared with a kind of anger at Uncle Robert. Then he had said, 'No!' and turned on his heel and walked away.

Now he saw Alix for himself. He spoke to her, and saw the expression of wistful anxiety that came at once to her face : she longed to understand what he said, and could not. Her gaze searched his face, but all she now saw were tears welling up in Alf's blue eyes. Uncle Robert laid a hand on his shoulder to take him aside. 'Alf! Alf!' he whispered. 'Your sadness will only make Alix unhappy.'

This was, however, the only time that Alf allowed his feelings to show. Like Aunt Elizabeth and Uncle Robert, he became steadily cheerful, trying always to interest Alix in new activities. Alix helped him in the garden, as Billy used to do. She also made him a reed pipe, and managed to teach him how to use it. Alf's delight was boundless.

One day he appeared with an eager face. He was carefully carrying a parcel which he said was for Alix. She was out with Sammy, so Alf set the parcel aside and began his gardening. At the usual time he broke off work for some cold tea with bread and cheese. He sat on an upturned tub, with the mysterious parcel by his side; and before the end of his break he could not resist undoing it. When Alix returned she found him, with his cheek still bulging with sandwich, gazing at a miniature caravan, brightly painted and complete with fat brown horse, which lay on his knees.

Alix stopped, transfixed with surprise, and charmed. With much pointing and other gesturing Alf made her understand that the little caravan and horse were his work, and were for her.

'Oh!' cried Alix, touching them almost reverently. 'They're lovely—lovely!'

'I made a little table and chair, too,' said Alf. 'Look! To go inside.'

'If only I could get little dolls to be gypsies in the caravan. . . .'

Aunt Elizabeth had come up behind Alix and now tapped her shoulder. Alix turned to see her Aunt nodding away and pointing towards the village. There they went together, at once. In the village shop, as Aunt Elizabeth had known, Alix found little wooden dolls of just about the right size. She bought three. Then, back at the house, she turned out Aunt Elizabeth's rag-bag to find bright scraps of material for skirts and shirts. She tied pieces of red silk over the dolls heads or round their throats as neckerchiefs.

During her stay Alix gradually added to her collection of things for the caravan. Some she made for herself; others she bought. The most useful was a little cooking-pot which could be hung on a tripod. Then, outside the caravan, Alix made a real fire under the pot, and cooked a real stew, using a little water, some gravy browning, a tiny onion, a runner bean, a slice of carrot—all the vegetables being cut into little pieces. She maintained to Alf—who said he preferred a stew with meat—that the gypsies evidently enjoyed their meals, because there was never any food left over. Actually Sammy cleared the tin plates in one lick, and the pot too, after which Alix carefully scoured it out, ready for next time.

Alix had endless fun with her caravan—fun that was

doing her more good than medicine. And she had decided to do something for Alf in return. After consultation with Aunt Elizabeth, she began work on an immense woollen sweater. It was to be knitted in a very intricate pattern in colours of orange, lemon and black. The choice of pattern and wools meant more shopping expeditions to the village. Alix arranged to buy an ounce of wool at a time, which she could manage from her pocket money. Aunt Elizabeth encouraged her to shop for herself, as she encouraged her in anything that helped her to regain confidence and venture out, as a deaf person, into the world of sound.

'She's doing well,' said Uncle Robert to Aunt Elizabeth, as they watched Alix trotting off for another ounce of wool. 'You must tell Edith.'

'Yes,' said Aunt Elizabeth. 'We help her—but—oh! I wish we could help her more—much, much more.'

14

In the Doldrums

At home, after Alix's departure, the Stacey family felt a sense of anti-climax. Things seemed flat and stale; and without Aunt Elizabeth and Alix even the house began to lose its look of freshness.

Christopher found himself in musical doldrums. He could neither interpret or create; and his music master, rightly guessing the cause to be the family upheaval over Alix, told him to leave his instruments for a while. 'Forget about them. You'll come back to them all right.' But Chris could feel no certainty of this.

Tessa, unlike Chris, practised with greater care than ever before. She somehow felt that she owed it to Alix, who had been deprived of her gift, to do the very best with her own. She was even advised to try for a scholarship at one of the colleges of music, but she refused, almost with annoyance.

'Even if I were lucky enough to get to a college, it would mean teaching in the end. And I couldn't. I've seen too much of it at home. Mother could wring some sort of music from a chimpanzee, but I'm not like mother. I'll take up nursing—all being well.'

'All being well' was an anxious phrase of Tessa's nowadays. Before Aunt Elizabeth left, she had had a private talk with Tessa. Gently she had pointed out that a nurse's job is so exacting that good health and strength can be as important for it as in professional music.

'But I must be a nurse, for Alix's sake,' protested Tessa. She was so near tears that Aunt Elizabeth said no more, except to say that there were many careers open to someone as intelligent and hard-working as Tessa could be.

'Don't bother your mother with doubts about your career,' she advised Tessa. 'There's still plenty of time to sort things out. And she has so many worries.'

So Tessa bore alone the thought of possible disappointment. She brooded and became depressed.

Only Billy remained his usual self, walking Chip, and keeping Alix's log cabin clean and swept.

As for Mr. and Mrs. Stacey, the strain of the months of Alix's illness, coupled with their usual professional work, told on them. They both looked careworn and older.

Mr. Stacey had once enjoyed the weekly choir practices in the church and the Sunday playing for the services; now he found them an increasing burden. One evening he said abruptly to Chris, 'I have been talking with the Vicar. I find the weekly choir practices and every Sunday playing for all the services rather much. If you agree, the Vicar and the choir are quite willing for you to take it. Not for always. Just to give me a break.'

Chris opened his mouth to refuse, then looked at his father. He felt a pang of contrition. Really, father did look tired, and—and *sagging*. He hesitated uneasily. He was a prefect at school and was not worried at the idea of dealing with the small boys in the choir; but the men, and the women—especially the women—frightened him.

'If you're sure the choir won't mind—' he began.

'I wouldn't ask you to do anything you couldn't undertake,' replied his father. 'Forget all about your age and think only of the music. If you try any innovations, you might get some opposition from some of the old hands, but if it seems right to you, don't take any notice.'

Chris, feeling cornered, rather resentfully said that he'd 'have a go.' He went to the church several times to take up his neglected organ practice so as to be ready for the first choir evening. When that evening came, he found that he was trembling. The small boys were inclined to play up, but Chris soon settled them by giving them his famous 'prefect's glare.'

The practices went off tolerably well, and after a time Chris dared to urge the choir to try an unaccompanied anthem by Palestrina. A few were enthusiastic, but the majority did not want the bother of learning something new to them. The singing was poor, and all at once Chris felt a boiling rage, not for himself, but for that perfectionist, his father. And for the composer whose lovely work was being mangled by carelessness.

He stopped them, and said very quietly, 'I know how difficult it is to get a proper balance. But you know, *you are just not listening to each other*. The basses are out-singing the altos and the sopranos are drowning everyone. It was awful.'

There was a dead silence, then a rustling of papers and a murmuring. Chris caught the words 'resign' and 'a boy of sixteen !'

Horribly conscious of smarting behind his eyelids, he said, 'It doesn't matter whether I'm sixteen or sixty. You accepted me as choir master, and choir master I must be, or the whole thing will fall to pieces. And no one can honestly say that the singing just now was good.'

One of the basses turned brick-red, and Chris half expected to be kicked through the vestry door. Instead, the man said, 'Christopher is quite right. We ought to back him up, and those who haven't a mind to had better say so now, and go home.'

Nobody moved, and Chris taking out a handkerchief and wiping his forehead, said, 'Thank you, sir. Now, will the basses sing their parts, and everybody else, softly humming their own parts, listen to them. Then we'll do the same with the altos and sopranos.'

It had been an uncomfortable ordeal for Chris, but it was the beginning of an absorbing hobby, which was to last him a lifetime.

Tessa, going into her mother's room one evening, found Alix's oboe in the wardrobe. She sat on the bed, the oboe's open case on her lap. The sudden discovery of the instrument had given her a feeling of bitter impotent rage. All her aspirations to help Alix seemed useless. Nothing could ease the burden her little sister had to bear.

In this mood Tessa sat there, tears which she made no attempt to control, pouring down her cheeks. Thus her mother found her.

Mrs.Stacey replaced the oboe in the wardrobe. 'Tessa, the boys are down by the stream. They miss Alix; don't let them miss you too. Dry your eyes and go to them. Quickly now.'

Tessa, ashamed, did as she was told, and at once began to feel less wretched. But she worried still, and now on account of her mother. In spite of her own distress she had suddenly noticed the *old* look on her mother's face. For the first time she had looked haggard.

'And I'm the daughter of the house now,' thought Tessa. 'I ought to be able to take care of her. I must.'

When Tessa arrived home from school the following

afternoon, she thought she would be alone in the house as usual. She was surprised to hear her mother's voice, calling from the bedroom. She found Mrs. Stacey in bed. Her face was colorless, and her damp hair clung on her forehead.

'Tessa, dear, I've had some sort of high temperature. I took some aspirins, and I feel the temperature has gone down. But I'm soaking wet with sweat. I tried getting out of bed, but—but I felt queer, and so giddy. I thought I'd better wait for you to help me to the bathroom.'

'Much better wash here,' said Tessa. She felt frightened, but tried hard to keep her head and think what needed to be done. She fetched towels and soap, a basin and a large jug of water. She helped her mother wash, slipped a clean nightdress over her head, and brushed and combed her hair. Then, clearing away the used things, she suggested a pot of tea.

'Oh, Tessa, it would be lovely! But what about—about supper for you and the boys?'

'Bother all that! Billy can scramble us some eggs and tomatoes. There's some cold meat, and I'll make father some sandwiches with that as he'll be late. Now, could you eat a lightly boiled egg?'

'I really think I could. I've had nothing all day.'

Tessa went down to the kitchen, and very soon reappeared carrying a tray. On it she had set a pot of tea, some thin bread and butter, a brown egg, and even two little rose buds in a potted meat jar.

'Now, if you feel like sitting in a chair and having this, I'll put some clean sheets on your bed.'

'This is wonderful,' sighed Mrs Stacey.

'Tomorrow's Saturday,' said Tessa, as she made the bed. 'Bed for you tomorrow, *and* Sunday, and Monday too if need be. Do you think I should ask the doctor to call?'

'No,' said Mrs. Stacey positively. 'I'm better already. But oh dear! What about tomorrow's pupils?'

'They can lump it for once. I'll telephone them this evening.' Tessa folded back a sheet. 'There—that's your bed done. Don't hurry. When you're ready, I'll help you back. I'll just go and see about father's sandwiches.'

Mrs. Stacey gave herself up to the luxury of being waited on, feeling cool, clean and rested. Left alone for a while, her gaze rested on the two late rosebuds, and her eyes filled. She had received many bouquets in her time, but none had touched her more deeply.

When Tessa came back, her mother said: 'I know that your own future seems far from clear to you, Tessa; but some things have become clear to me. You may or may not be able to become a nurse, after all; but you will always be able to help those who are ill. It is a great gift.'

Tessa stared at her mother, amazed. 'But—but I've only been doing the obvious things that needed doing.'

'To see what needs doing and to do it—that's what I mean, exactly.'

15

Family Visit

The next day Mrs. Stacey's temperature was below normal, but she felt drowsy and weak. A letter came for her from Aunt Elizabeth, and Tessa carried it upstairs, prepared not only to open it but to read it aloud. But her mother, with her eyes closed, said, 'Don't bother; I'll read it properly later. Just tell me if there's anything important in it.'

'Um . . . um . . .' Tessa began to scan the letter. 'Oh, good old Aunt Elizabeth! She's never thought of such a thing before!'

Mrs. Stacey opened her eyes. 'What?'

'She says why don't we *all* go down for a weekend. She says we three can cram into the house with Alix, but you'd be more comfortable in Alf's mother's spare bedroom in the village.'

'And Alix—how is she?' Mrs. Stacey's interest was sharpening.

'Taken up sketching. Hopes to do a full length—horizontal length, I suppose—of Sammy. . . . Oh, it would be lovely if we all went, as Aunt Elizabeth says. Isn't it *nice* of her? But she is nicer than she used to be. She seems to have changed somehow, since Alix's illness.'

'She's trying to help,' said Mrs. Stacey. 'Like all of us. Oh, Tessa, why did it have to be Alix. Why couldn't it have

been me? It would have been so much easier to bear.' Mrs.
Stacey, turning her head on her pillow, wept.

Tessa felt that a fortress had crumbled. She could only
sit silently, holding her mother's hand. Then, realizing that
she would rather be left alone, she went out of the room.
She felt tired and beaten. Lonely too. All the others happened to be out. The house seemed empty as never before.
'It's not home any more. It's just four walls and a roof,'
thought Tessa.

Soon she made herself go back to her mother's room. She
found that her mother, too, had made an effort. She was
sitting up, her hair freshly combed and even her face
powdered—rather blotchily. She smiled and began to talk
cheerfully of plans for the visit to Aunt Elizabeth. For it
was soon settled: they would all go for the first possible
weekend.

The news of the forthcoming visit overjoyed Alix. She,
too, had felt a strange new loneliness, although it was of a
different kind from Tessa's. During the day at Aunt
Elizabeth's she found so much to occupy her, and she had
the entire responsibility of Sammy. Since she had lost her
hearing, the other senses seemed to have sharpened. Uncle
Robert noticed her new interest in his use of colors in
painting, and with what intentness she now watched the
flight of birds and other natural movements. Sometimes she
sniffed the air, rather like Sammy himself, as if to get some
clue to what was happening.

But at night Alix was lonely. Then there was the great
silence, darkness, the cold stars and herself. And she could
not rap on the wall for her mother now.

One night the oppressive loneliness became more than
she could bear. She got out of bed to go she didn't quite
know where. Perhaps into the garden, among the roses,

pale and dark, and the pinks, and the clear grass. She put on her dressing gown, and opened her bedrom door. Immediately there bounded into her arms a soft, energetic creature, who pleaded, with all the wriggles at his command, to be allowed to stay.

'Oh, Sammy,' Alix whispered. 'I ought to take you straight back to the kitchen!' Instead, she took him to bed, and soon they were both asleep.

In the morning, there was no need for confession : the moment Aunt Elizabeth came into Alix's room, Sammy hopped out of bed and scampered downstairs to be let out.

Alix could read Aunt Elizabeth's mind in her face. A dog in bed—how unhygenic! And then there was the possibility of fleas. . . . Yet at the same moment Aunt Elizabeth had a sudden remembrance of her first term at boarding school, when, clamped down by rules, and shut off from her beloved woods and meadows, she had suffered an agony of homesickness. . . . She could guess at what Alix felt, and what Sammy's warm presence meant to her.

So Aunt Elizabeth smiled, and Alix knew that she and Sammy had won. Sammy was thoroughly inspected for fleas—Aunt Elizabeth insisted on that. (No need, really, Alix kept him so well-groomed). Then he had the right to go to bed every night curled into Alix's arms. And Alix slept. She could not feel lost, or lonely, or cut-off with Sammy, who did not know that she was suffering from any of these things.

So Sammy was with Alix night and day. He gambolled about her on her walks and shopping expeditions to the village; he lay patiently and watched when she worked beside Alf in the garden or bent over her gypsies and their caravan.

'That dog's devoted to Alix,' said Uncle Robert, watching them together.

'More important, she's devoted to him,' said Aunt Elizabeth. 'He can't speak and she can't hear; but they don't need that kind of communication, anyway.'

There were only a very few occasions on which Sammy ever left Alix's side : a mouse in the long grass would distract and detain him; the sight of Captain McIvor—who seldom deigned to set foot in the garden—would chain him to the spot he stood on, respectfully whispering his growls. Other dogs he never saw.

'It'll be lovely to see him with Chip,' Alix told them. 'They really play together, although Chip bosses him around, being older. Oh, it will be lovely to see Billy with Chip, and Tessa, and all of them !'

At home the Stacey family, too, were in a state of high anticipation of their forthcoming visit to Aunt Elizabeth. They had heard that the room in Mrs.Stevens' cottage was ready. Suitcases had been brought down from the Stacey attic; clothes washed and ironed and mended—Tessa saw to a good many of the arrangements. The house was to be left in Mrs.Bullock's care : she had her instructions and a spare key of the house.

The day before they were due to leave the barometer in the hall stood at 'Set Fair,' but the sky was grey.

'Oh, if only the weather holds !' said Billy. He was giving Chip an extra grooming before the reunion with Sammy .

'Early to say yet,' said Mr. Stacey. 'You can't tell what will happen tomorrow.'

And down at Aunt Elizabeth's, Alf was trying to tell Alix much the same thing, although he watched skies and trees and birds, not a barometer.

'You never know,' said Alf, and wagged his head doubtfully. 'The Lord sends different weather for different pur-
poses.' He certainly did not want Alix's time with her family
to be spoilt; but on the other hand the garden needed rain,
after a dry spell. He was having to water some plants to
save their lives.

'Anyway, if it does rain, we can still enjoy ourselves indoors,' said Alix. 'And I know you'd like rain, Alf. Can I
come with you to the well house?' That was where Alf
was going now, to fetch water.

Sammy was away on some expedition, so Alix went alone
with Alf into the well-house.

As she entered, she could scarcely see anything. Then
her eyes became accustomed to the dark and she saw the
one tiny window, overshadowed with ivy. Rakes and bean
poles and a twig broom stood in a corner. She saw them
on the far side of the well itself, with its strong chain and
dangling bucket, and the low, mossy wall which surrounded
it.

Alix went to the wall and leaned her hands on it. Her
eyes were quite used to the twilight now, and she looked
down with fascinated horror at the dreadful depths which
sunk in a green and slimy tunnel, down and down. You
could only just glimpse a dark glint of water far below.

'Best to come away now,' said Alf.

Alix, of course, did not hear him, but without knowing
it, she almost answered him : 'I must just drop in one
stone, and see the splash.'

She did not hear the eager barking of Sammy from outside; Alf did, but thought nothing of it. Sammy was coming at a great and joyful pace to find his mistress. The door
of the well house stood open and his nose told him she was
inside.

Alix was stooping to find her stone when Sammy burst in. He was excited and quick. He rushed round the well house, sniffing; then scrabbled up the little wall to see what was the other side, lost his footing, and disappeared into the well.

16

A New Song

It had all happened so quickly. One moment Alf was taking a pace towards the well and Alix was stooping for her stone; the next, Sammy had gone.

Alix screamed : 'Sammy ! What shall we do? What shall we— The bucket ! Alf, the bucket—you must let me down in the bucket ! Do as I tell you !'

But Alf, who had seldom moved so fast, was already doing as Alix told him; he had complete faith in her at this moment. Alix had seized the chain to clamber into the bucket. 'Let me down slowly, and stop the very moment I shout.'

She was in, with Alf's help, and Alf cautiously released the catch. 'Slowly, Alf. . . .'

Slowly, slowly Alf was letting down the precious burden. His teeth were gritted together, and sweat began to pour from his face. At the end of its chain the bucket swung pendulum like, grazing Alix's knuckles first against one wet wall, then against the other. Alix felt herself falling slowly, but still falling . . . falling . . . falling. All the terrors of her falling dreams came back to her, overwhelmed her. Then the thought of Sammy below swept everything else from her mind.

She could see him now, swimming desperately round, pawing for any foothold at the sides of the well. She was near the water herself now; and nearer; and nearer. . . .

She shouted '*Stop!*' and the bucket ceased its descent and hung over the blackness. Crouching, gripping the chain with one hand, she reached out and downwards with the other and caught Sammy by the scruff. For a moment girl and dog seemed to be struggling together in battle, for Sammy was panic-stricken and Alix desperate. Then she managed to haul him to her and he suddenly realized that here, even in this dark darkness, there was safety. He lay still against her.

Another shout to Alf, and the ascent began. Alix had now only one hand for the chain, the other clutched the wet and trembling puppy to her breast. She shut her eyes and prayed inwardly : 'Please, God, let Alf bring us to the top. Don't let his strength give way.'

She was aware of some difference around her, and realized it seemed lighter. They were nearing the top of the wall. Alf's brawny arm came out and held them, and Alix knew that she and Sammy were safe. She heard Alf say, 'Don't try to get out.'

Still holding the winch with one hand, he lifted Alix and Sammy out, over the little wall of the well, and on to the beaten earth floor of the well house.

It was not until they were outside in the sunshine—Alf and Alix between laughing and crying, Sammy bounding and yelping—that Alix realized that she had *heard* Alf speak. From the moment she had known they were safe again, she had heard every sound. . . .

She stopped, turned abruptly to Alf, and told him. He was silent some time, as if in awe; then he thanked the Lord.

They told Aunt Elizabeth and Uncle Robert. The doctor was called, and when he had seen Alix and confirmed the miraculous recovery, Uncle Robert telephoned the Staceys.

He conveyed as best he could the doctor's explanation : that the ordeal—the shock and the danger in the well house—had restored Alix's hearing. The family could hardly understand the explanation, but they did understand the great fact of Alix's recovery. She herself spoke on the telephone and asked for her oboe to be brought down the next day.

Each member of the Stacey family reacted to the news in his or her own way. Chris went into the church and almost split the roof with his triumphant playing of Bach. Mrs. Stacey went up to her room and remained there a long time, alone. Tessa saw to the supper, with extra care. Billy polished Chip's collar and lead, and groomed Chip himself with such vigour that it was a wonder a hair of his coat was left.

Mr. Stacey was the only one who could not choose what to do. He had to play in a concert that evening. He had a solo part. People in the front rows of the audience wondered why tears were pouring down his cheeks, but the conductor, a huge Dutchman, knew. Afterwards, in the artist's room, he gave him a great hug. The members of the orchestra were less demonstrative, but everyone seemed to be offering Mr. Stacey cigarettes and wanting to shake him by the hand.

At Aunt Elizabeth's, Alix had gone to bed early—the doctor had recommended caution. She lay awake, but felt she was in a dream. The appearance of everything was just as it had been last night—the garden; the hills, shadowy against the clear sky; the stars; the trees. But oh ! now there were *sounds* too. A rustling of leaves and grass. The soft reedy note of a little owl. Sammy's snorting as he twisted on the bed.

And Alix remembered what Alf had said so quietly when,

outside the well house, he realized that she could hear. He had said a wonderful thing. . . .

The next day the Staceys came, brimming over with excitement and gladness at the unexpectedly happy reunion.

That day seemed timeless: it was filled with ordinary activities, yet each person felt that nothing could be quite ordinary again. Suitcases were taken to Mrs. Stevens' cottage, and there and at Aunt Elizabeth's the unpacking was done. Then Alix's paintings had to be examined, and the caravan exclaimed over. Meanwhile, Aunt Elizabeth was working quietly at the preparation of meals and supervising the necessary routine of the day. She was most reliably helped by Tessa. 'How the child seems to have changed!' whispered Uncle Robert, and Aunt Elizabeth smiled.

Her oboe had been restored to Alix, and she took it outside into the garden so that Alf could hear her playing her first little tune. Her face was intent and joyful as she played.

After supper that evening, when they were all gathered in the sitting room, they talked at length of the miraculous recovery. Alix leant against her mother, with Sammy on her knee. In a lull of conversation she said almost awkwardly: 'I can't think now why I ever thought of being anything but a musician. It was silly of me. Now I know: I must play my oboe.'

There was a long silence in which Mr. and Mrs. Stacey smiled at each other: a dream had come true. Christopher said, 'Good!' and Billy blinked in wonderment. Only Tessa seemed puzzled—almost upset.

'But you wanted to be a nurse. . . .'

'Not now.'

'But I'd decided I must be a nurse because you couldn't be. . . .'

All Tessa's ideas were suddenly topsy-turvy.

Mrs. Stacey said gently : 'Perhaps you will be a nurse still, Tessa; but it will have to be because *you* want it and because it suits *you* as a career. Not because of Alix. Everyone must live their own life.'

Tessa nodded slowly : 'Yes, yes. . . . That's true. . . .' Her thoughtful frown vanished; she lifted her face, bright with joy for Alix : 'And Alix's life is music after all; and it *can* be, since she can hear again.'

This was the chance Alix had been waiting for. She went back to the story of the rescue and the well house, and told them for the first time what Alf had said when they had come outside again and were looking at each other over the soaked, cheerful Sammy.

'When he knew I could hear, Alf said, "Oh, sing unto the Lord a new song!" And I never knew that an ordinary face could look so—so—'

'Joyful?'

'More than that. Don't laugh—Alf's face looked beautiful.'

No one felt the least inclination to laugh, and after a moment : ' "Sing unto the Lord a new song," ' repeated Chris. 'Father let me try. I'll write something for piano, cello, violin, contralto, *and oboe*.'